Copyright

I

Dedication(s)

To my Mother, Margaret H. Williams (1909-1988) with all my love.

To David Shadrick for his help, friendship, and encouragement.

CHASING THE SPIDER

D.S. Mitchell

Fire Mountain Media

Vancouver   Portland

www.chasingthespider.com

IV

Chapter One

Ten Most Wanted

My name is Sky Evenson. If you've been watching any of the cable news shows, chances are you've heard my name, and those of my two friends, Cory Davis, and Ward Haskins. We're fugitives.

Ten months ago, I was a senior at Lake Oswego High School and star forward on the Girls' Varsity basketball team. I was recruited by Yale and Pepperdine. I had big plans for a career in genetic research and had decided to do my undergrad work at Yale and play basketball for them.

Ward Haskins was Rally King, and class clown. As such he was one of the most popular kids in school. Despite his crazy antics, he was a terrific student and had been accepted at Northwestern. He was expected to join his father's law practice after graduation.

Cory Davis was the stepson of Jerry Johnson, the sitting U.S. Congressman for Oregon's Fifth District. Johnson has served for the past decade as Speaker of the House of Representatives. Cory was an honor student and Class AAA State Heavyweight Wrestling Champion. Courted by USC, Cory was set to enter their International Studies program in the fall. He was headed to a career in the U.S. Diplomatic Service.

I'm sure you're wondering how three kids from Northwest affluence ended up on the FBI's 10 Most Wanted List. It began with hatred and obsession and it ended in murder and flight to avoid prosecution.

I should have been able to do something to change the course of events, but I didn't know then what I know now. I hadn't yet suffered the pain of decisions made in haste. I was caught in the undertow of other people's actions, trying not to be swept away, trying to keep my head above water.

I've replayed it over and over, looking for any new angle. A grim incident, always ready for instant replay. I am forever caught in the same tragic loop. Like Rosencrantz and Guildenstern, plus one.

After I tell you what happened that weekend in June, it will be up to you to decide what I could have done differently.

Since leaving home, I have out of necessity and circumstance, changed my appearance. I don't think my parents would recognize me.

I've cropped my once waist length hair short. Very, short. Bleached white, struck through with luminous highlighting strips of aqua blue and green. Reckless confusion. Ragged spikes explode across the crown of my head, with jagged shards, hugging my face. All angles and agitated turmoil, my hair a reflection of my life.

I was down thirty-five pounds and had the look of a meth addict with deep circles under wary eyes. My weight loss a result of being chained to a treadmill of terror. High doses of Adrenalin had my body on hyper-alert, ready to run at the first whiff of trouble.

I tried not to look in the mirror. I no longer recognized the emaciated person staring back at me, with vacant eyes, and unknown future.

The hardest thing for me to disguise was my ridiculous height. 5'10" in bare feet. I was the only girl in the entire state that could regularly pull off a dunk.

I'd always been proud of my height, but now it was a feature difficult to hide. I'd taken to wearing flats and had developed a permanent slouch. I tried to remain seated whenever possible. I also tried to associate myself with the tallest people in the room. Staying on the periphery of the activity, using perspective to my advantage.

I was in Chandler, Texas, working at the El Sombrero Motel as a part-time maid and desk clerk. With my paycheck, and the few extra bucks I take from the cash-drawer, I knew I'd be okay money wise for a while.

I stole so little it wouldn't be worth filling out a police report. I wasn't out to break anyone. They probably wouldn't even know there had been a theft.

I had a good car and new ID, procured from a creative small-time forger. Jimmy T. specialized in providing papers for the stream of illegals that came north, looking for work, not terrified teenagers running for their lives.

Jimmy was tall with sculptured features and almond skin and a raw sexual intensity that unnerved me. His English was British boarding-school perfect. He was exotically handsome, with black eyes and full lips. I have no idea how old he was, though he looked about thirty-five.

He called himself Jimmy T., but I was sure that wasn't his real name. No serious adult called themselves Jimmy. Of course, I was in Texas. He told me he was born in Khartoum, Sudan. Maybe. Maybe, not. I now assume, everyone who opens their mouth to speak, is lying.

The name of that distant place however fueled my imagination. A blue tiled world of mystery and intrigue. Narrow twisting streets, mosques and muezzins, shrouded secrets, and clandestine operations. Robe clad princes on majestic stallions and erotic Arabian nights filled my dreams. The fragrance of jasmine and patchouli enveloped me.

Wherever he came from, was his business. But I had to admit, Khartoum seemed more appropriate for a document purveyor than Hoboken.

Jimmy talked in a near whisper. That habit required me to lean close, straining to hear what he was saying. He smelled of bakhoor, saffron and cinnamon. There was a raw sensuality between us. He left me breathless.

I wondered if he suspected a wire, or just wanted a chance to brush against me? Whatever his motive, I liked his attentiveness.

Jimmy claimed he had developed a state-of-the-art method to alter photos. Just enough to escape facial recognition technology. He showed me how with just the slightest computer manipulation, the picture would be too vague to raise suspicion. The photos coming up clear of outstanding warrants.

"Unfortunately, Miss Lori," he cautioned, "if authorities decide to photograph you and then scan that photo," he said with a fatalist motion of his hands, "you're toast."

It was an extra $250 on the sticker price but I jumped at it, keen to have another weapon in my arsenal of illicit tools and tactics.

Chapter Two

Hot Shower

San Antonio was a hot 297 miles from Chandler, and the drive took me just over four hours. I stopped a couple of times to pee and stretch. Thanks to great air conditioning the drive wasn't bad.

I listened to Eminem, Jay Z, Shakira and Lizzo the first hundred miles. As I moved further south, I switched to the driving sounds of Heavy Metal, Sabbath, Motorhead, Stratovarius. Sometimes I need a push, and the right kind of music can do that for me. I especially like the old European heavy metal stuff, recorded thirty years before I was born.

My border crossing goal was Brownsville and its good highway into the heart of Mexico. To tell the truth, I wasn't in any great hurry. Thank Zeus I hadn't seen my high school yearbook picture flashed on a TV screen in weeks. That might be one of the reasons I was in no hurry to leave the USA.

Scary things can happen in Mexico. I was aware of that. Kidnapping, rape, and murder are commonplace. Not usually to Americanos, but anyone in the wrong place at the wrong time can end up at the mercy of a Mexican drug smuggler or sex trafficker. Of course, being snagged by bounty hunters or the Federales could be just as bad.

The price on my pretty little head seemed to grow with every news flash. Last time I saw a reward amount, it was $150,000. That's one hell of a lot of pesos. Whatever the dangers in Mexico, my list of choices was short and growing shorter.

So far, the time I spent away from the United States had been voluntary. Two summers in France for a French Emersion program. One year in Provence, the other in Paris. Then there were two summers in Mexico. One in Mexico City and one providing health care services to farm workers in Jalisco State.

But this departure was different, I realized I might never come home, and if I did it would most likely be in shackles, or possibly a coffin.

When I played with the idea of going south, I was convinced that anyone who knew my history was aware I was fluent in Spanish and French. I figured the police would assume Mexico would be my most likely destination. Or less likely, but still a possibility would be Eastern Canada. Even though the French in Paris and the French in Montreal and Moncton being vastly different. Any place in French speaking Canada could provide a refuge.

Whether headed north or south I believed the authorities thought that I had already left the United States. That didn't mean I thought crossing the border now would be easy. I expected the check points to be on high alert. I found

7

myself wishing I had left the country immediately after the murders. I had had over 24 hours to make that crossing. Totally possible if I'd only known.

I was optimistic the drastic change in my appearance, scan proof I.D., and fluent Spanish would simplify things. It's easier getting into Mexico than getting back into the US, especially if you are a fugitive with your picture decorating every post office in the country.

My greatest fear was technology. Particularly facial recognition. Though if Jimmy T. had done what he promised, I'd be golden.

Lies, conspiracy, and thievery, have become my go to solutions. I've learned that circumstances really can bend a person's moral compass. Everything I was ever taught about honesty and truth now contradicted by life.

I found a small adobe style motel close to the town center and paid for one night. I guessed that the Little Alamo Motel had been built in the 1940's. The classic adobe exterior surrounded by greenery. Lush palms, avocado, and fig trees and huge hanging flower baskets. Outside of each room sat a large terra cotta pot overflowing with flowers. Charming comes to mind.

I pulled the Sportage into a shaded parking spot and unloaded a minimum of clothes and hygiene paraphernalia. Stashing my stuff in the room, I cranked the air conditioner to high. I kicked off my shoes and laid down on the bed. I debated whether I should shower now, or later. Later.

The River Walk was crowded with shoppers and sightseers. Lush foliage, towering Cypress, Oaks, and Willows shaded the walkways. Water taxis filled the river. The sounds of Latin guitar strains danced on the air and primary colors sparked a joyous mood.

I found a seat under a red and yellow umbrella at a sidewalk café and ordered a coffee and watched the river traffic. Loneliness now my constant companion. I wished Cory and Ward were with me. I was feeling the isolation of the road. I just wanted someone to touch me. Hug me. I was certainly short of my share of hugs recently. But the likelihood of intimate contact was shrinking by the day.

It was nearly dark as I walked back to the motel. I was tired and hot, and was ready for a shower and truthfully, I didn't know where else to go. Thank Zeus I had left the air conditioner on full blast, it was a welcome relief from the Texas heat.

The glow from the television filled the room with flickering light. I ran through two dozen channels before my growling stomach spurred me to action. Checking my phone, I found a local pizza joint and ordered a medium sized Supreme with extra cheese

I dropped on the bed and took a deep breath and closed my eyes and slid unexpectedly into sleep.

The terror hit with solid knocks. I struggled to inhale. For a terrible moment I wasn't sure I could breathe.

"Domino's Pizza. Hot to your door!"

The third knock stimulated my limbs to movement, forcing my feet to the carpeted floor.

"Hey, I ain't got all night."

Before opening the door, I made a quick surveillance of my reflection in the mirror, assuring myself that Sky Evenson, fugitive killer, bore no resemblance to the ghostly, shadowed occupant of room #112.

I opened the door to a dazzling smile. The pizza guy was about my age, tall and thin with sandy hair, and dancing grey eyes. He watched me with an amused grin as I dug through my purse for my wallet. My eyes were drawn to his perfectly rounded ass and his hands which were free of a wedding ring.

He gave me a lingering smile as I handed over $20 and told him to keep the change. I wondered if he ever hooked up with customers. I suspected that he wouldn't miss a beat if I gave him the right signals.

I leaned against the door jam, pizza in hand and watched him jog back to his truck. He crawled behind the wheel and turned on the engine before he looked up and locked eyes with mine. He hesitated and bit his lip before giving me a slight nod and a quick peace sign before hitting the road.

I sat alone and ate three slices of the pizza. It was hot and filled the empty hole in my stomach.

The pretty boy with the amazing smile re-entered my thoughts. Closing my eyes, I focused on him. I stifled a giggle. I would certainly, never see him again. Which was probably why I was thinking about him and his sweet ass.

My cotton shirt dropped easily off my shoulders, as I imagined the Domino's stud was there with me. I was still a virgin, though not for a lack of trying. That was what I told myself anyway. It had just never been the right person, or the right place or time. I knew sex wasn't a space launch, but I still wanted it to be right for my first time.

However, if I was going to die, or, spend the rest of my life in prison, I wanted to shed the innocence of childhood. Something I was already on my way to doing, by circumstance, if not design. Recently, I had experienced a growing inferno of sexual curiosity, pushing me toward experimentation.

11

I turned the shower to high and stepped into intentionally cool water, raising goosebumps on my bare skin. Soaping a washcloth, I started to scrub. Washing off the Texas dirt that had sunk into every pore.

My breath caught in my throat, as I imagined him kissing my breasts. Practiced hands gently tugging each nipple. His sweet sucking and licking. My breath came back in ragged gulps. I opened my eyes and was greeted with dazzling grey eyes.

He pressed his body against mine, drawing a soft gasp from me. At an unhurried pace, he moved his tongue deep into my mouth. All the while his hands caressing my ears, moving slowly and gently down along the side of my neck. Soft guttural moans the sound and rhythm of our passion.

His hand moved down my abdomen raising every fine hair on my body. As I reached out to him, he took both of my arms, securing them at the wrist. Tethered together, with his eyes burning into me, he raised my arms above my head. I felt a gentle burn run through me from the light stress position. A smile touched my lips.

His gaze remained locked on mine, while his free hand moved across the threshold of my mons and into my tight slit. I jerked convulsively as his eyes flashed.

I swam helplessly in a sea of desire. I wanted to wrap my arms around him, but they were occupied. My lover resisting any thought of releasing them.

With my arms still held above my head he brought his fingers to his mouth and sucked on them, and with a carnal growl whispered close to my ear, "You taste like my favorite candy."

Our eyes are locked in a blaze of intimate excitement. He let my arms fall to my sides and I reached for him, taking his hard organ in both hands. Moving my hands, up and down his throbbing shaft, I felt his passion intensify. I stroked slowly at first, but then started to pump more rapidly as I watched his reaction.

He grabbed me by the hips and rubbed his erection against my body. I felt my face flush as we groaned in the agony of pleasure.

The water was still running and my response to his continued stimulation was mounting. I felt his fingers slip into the mouth of my vagina and I was overwhelmed with passion.

When I opened my eyes the man with the dancing grey eyes and the pouty mouth had vanished. I laughed finding my own hand at the threshold of my sex.

My heart pounded as I moved my lathered fingers on to my clit, aggressively stimulating myself. Pressing myself firmly against the tile of the shower stall, my release exploded

13

like shattering glass. It took me a minute, but I slowly regained my senses and shut off the shower.

I hitched the bath towel around my waist and grabbed a second one to dry my hair. I ran the towel repeated through my hair until it was semi-dry. My nervous fingers untangled the damp mess and brought it under control.

I settled in to watch *'Breaking Bad,'* but I tired of its dark tone quickly and was soon pawing amongst the visitor's brochures, bedding, and damp towels searching for the always illusive TV remote.

I settled on a local news station, just as pictures of Cory, Ward, and me flashed on the screen. Our pictures were dramatically enlarged and hovered behind the baby-faced TV news anchor as he gave an update on the man hunt for three Oregon teens. The story he told was highly fictionalized and thus intentionally grizzly. The tale of murder, computer hacking, and Chinese spying, more appropriate for a Tom Clancy novel than real life.

Breathing is an involuntary response. One of the most basic vital functions. The primitive portion of the brain known as the Medulla regulates such basic functions. Knowing this didn't change the fact that I couldn't breathe.

I doubt there are any reliable statistics to the phenomenon, but I'd wager at least one person dies every day from one terror or another.

The News Bulletin closed, and an ad for dental implants came on screen permitting my diaphragm to relax from its constricted seizure, just in time for me to take a gulp of life saving oxygen.

Chapter Three

Mateo

I ebbed between sleep and wakefulness. Restless images from the television flickered eerily across walls and furniture. I was somewhere between a dream and a nightmare when the volume level amplified the voice of a well-known pitchman for the after-midnight shoppers.

I rolled over, ignoring the salesman's annoying voice. It was still dark outside. Despite my exhaustion I let the television play. I needed its irritating sound. I needed its aggravating company.

The previous year I'd toured the amazing round pyramid sites in Mexico's Jalisco state with my Aunt Janet. Janet is a Nurse Practitioner who was in Mexico on a government sponsored mission providing health care services for agricultural workers in rural areas of the country. She had arranged to take me along as her government paid nursing assistant.

In Mexico, police activities often use the combined services of the federal, state, and municipalities. You will often be confronted by open trucks with agents from the three separate services carrying automatic weapons and you had better take them seriously.

That afternoon, a year ago, the police had cars pulled over at a roadblock and were in the process of doing extensive searches. Drugs and gun smuggling are big business in Mexico and each vehicle was being searched for illegal contraband.

I'm convinced bigtime criminals aren't driving up and down the roads of Mexico in the family station wagon. The drugs and guns are going through major airports or hidden in 18 wheelers that travel between the two countries, or tunnels two lanes wide under the streets of San Diego and every other major border city.

Truthfully, the roadblocks and the traffic stops are nothing more than theater, designed to create a perception that something is being done, without doing anything.

As we sat on the roadside waiting for instructions an incredibly good-looking young officer, in the dark blue uniform of the State Police leaned in our car window. He looked at Aunt Janet, and then at me. His gaze hovered on me, making me self-conscious. Was it the skimpy bikini top or the short shorts, I wondered?

He flashed a magazine perfect smile. I couldn't see his eyes hidden behind his aviators. In perfect American English he asked us to show our papers. The always ready Janet quickly produced her documents and handed them over for him to review.

I wasn't as prepared as my aunt and was forced to get out of the passenger seat of Janet's rented Jeep and walk to the back hatch to search for my identification.

The young officer, his automatic weapon casually slung over his left shoulder followed close behind me. I could feel his eyes on my ass.

He was tall, at least six two. He was so close I could smell his aftershave. I felt a sigh escape, and realized my hands were trembling and prayed he had not linked my nervousness to his overt sexuality.

Good-looking guys don't usually unsettle me, but he was movie star handsome, and he was standing so fucking close to me, I could hardly think. He watched my every move, as I dug amongst the bags and suitcases, including my soiled laundry, until I found the elusive documents. When I looked up, I realized he was looking down the front of my bikini top. To be fair, I was spilling out of the damn thing.

"Are you staying in Guadalajara?" he asked, his concentration focused on my chest.

"The La Paloma Inn."

He handed back my passport and visa documents. When he didn't release them immediately, I knew he was teasing me, although I didn't know why.

18

"A pleasure meeting you, Miss Evenson," he said, finally releasing my paperwork.

I felt my head bob up and down.

"Thank you," I said quietly, now delivering intense concentration to my feet.

Raising my eyes, I caught my aunt's quizzical gaze in the Jeep's rearview mirror.

His voice drew my attention back to him, "I'd like to take you and your companion to dinner. Would you allow me to take you where us locals go when we want a great meal?"

I felt my jaw go slack. It took a second to get control of my galloping heart.

"We'd love to. We are in room #139 at the La Paloma Inn."

He hesitated, delivering me another of his mind-bending smiles. Seconds began to feel like minutes. My palms sweaty and my mouth as dry as a hangover.

After a period of serious thought, he finally volunteered, "In case you're interested, my name is Mateo, Captain Mateo Rios."

Pink faced I said, "I'm happy to meet you, Mateo."

Embarrassed, yet gleefully happy for the unexpected invitation, I turned and walked back around the Jeep, shaking like a schoolgirl who had just met Justin Bieber or Nick Jonas. I slid into the passenger seat and buckled my seat belt. I turned to Janet and nearly blinded her with a toothy full-faced grin.

Captain Rios walked back to the driver's side of the car and engaged Janet in conversation, "I saw medical supplies and equipment in the back of your vehicle."

"Yes, sir. I'm a Nurse Practitioner. My niece and I will be working with the farmers in Jalisco state. Before starting our assignment, we wanted to play like tourists."

With a nearly imperceptible nod of his head, Captain Mateo Rios acknowledged her response, and with another of those gorgeous smiles, said, "In that case, we won't delay you any longer. My apologies, Senorita."

I sat spellbound, watching as Captain Rios motioned our vehicle back onto the highway pavement. He signaled the officer manning the roadblock that the Jeep was free to go without search, with a simple one-word explanation, "Medico."

Believe me, we were ecstatic. If you've ever been stopped at a Mexican roadblock you know what I mean. The process can take hours and if you are unlucky, you may end up with everything you own sitting outside your vehicle in the dirt while authorities poke, prod and investigate every interior space of your vehicle, while repeatedly scrutinizing your documents over, and over again, for any irregularities or suggestion of forgery.

As we headed back to town, I told Janet that the Captain had asked us to have dinner with him.

She delivered a knowing smile, "I thought something was going on between you two."

I wrapped my arms around my knees, dragging them close to my chest and squealed like an adolescent.

"I think he's the best-looking guy I've ever seen."

"Well, he certainly is handsome. I think he felt obligated to take me along."

Janet is my mother's younger sister and was a late addition to my grandparent's life plan. Janet is barely ten years older than I am, and by the way, is drop dead gorgeous.

"What time?" Janet asked.

"Oh my, I forgot to ask. I could barely remember the name of the hotel. He must think I'm a complete idiot!"

Somewhere between him walking up to our car and his invitation to dinner I had lost my senior cool and calm nonchalance. I had, in front of this hunk of masculinity turned into what I was, an inexperienced girl in the throes of flowering womanhood.

21

At 7 o'clock the front desk called and told Janet a gentleman was waiting for us in the lobby.

Janet gave me a quick look of approval. I had showered and changed from the bikini top and short shorts, into a gauzy white dress, complemented by a beautiful coral and turquoise necklace and matching earrings that I had bought in Mexico City the previous year.

"Do you think I'm overdressed?" I asked.

"You look exquisite. He'll be the one that can't breathe tonight," she reassured me.

I gave her a hug for so quickly restoring my confidence.

Mateo turned to face us as we crossed the tiled lobby. He was even better looking in a crisp white shirt, and perfectly tailored charcoal slacks than he had been in his uniform. His aviators were pushed back on his head, and for the first time I saw his beautiful green eyes.

His gaze, bold and unapologetic, turned my knees to jelly. I felt my lungs take a small gasp as I felt my cheeks warm.

"Good evening, ladies," Mateo said, giving us a formal bow.

Mateo first nodded to Janet and smiled, before locking eyes with mine, sending a visible quiver through my body.

He led us through the two-story high lobby and into the early evening sunset, just in time to watch the last moments of daylight hover on the horizon, sending red and gold shards across our faces and everything around us. It was magical.

He had chosen Casa del Rios for dinner. The restaurant was a beautiful, converted mission, owned by his cousin, Raul Rios. Raul was round faced and jovial. Although the restaurant was busy, Raul was exceptionally attentive to our table. He was full of stories of his life in kitchens around the world. We all laughed when he told us, "the French are spoiled pussies, and the Italians arrogant bastards, and the Brits are as cold as cod."

"What about Americans? Janet asked.

"I love Americans. The women are the most beautiful in the world."

"All of them?" Janet pressed.

"Of course. I'm a democrat when it comes to love."

Mateo told us his parents met and married in Seattle, Washington. He was a West Coaster like me. His mother was an academic. She was a professor of Psychology at U. of W.

His father was a Mexican national and was part of the Mexican Embassy delegation in Seattle.

Mateo had grown up on Alki Beach, part of trendy West Seattle. He told us he had spent every summer in Mexico since he could walk. He had transplanted to his father's homeland after graduating from Fordham University the previous spring with majors in Political Science and Pre-Law.

The Mexican government had been offering large bonuses to entice bilingual college educated individuals into the military and state police. In fact, when the cost of living was considered, he said going south offered him an opportunity that far exceeded anything in the United States, without three more years of school.

With his father's government contacts Mateo was looking to a future in politics. He said that more than anything he wanted to help the poor and underserved of Mexico and the United States. He told us he had continued his education taking classes online from Fordham and expected to challenge the New York bar exam the coming spring.

"Are you planning on going back to New York?" Janet asked.

"I like to keep my options open. Life is fluid," he said, his eyes twinkling, "I love New York."

Mateo was easy, idealistic, and motivated. Janet was funny and smart and kept the conversation moving. I was thankful for Janet's presence. For my part, I mostly had lock jaw. I had to concentrate on not staring at Mateo, while consciously ignoring my heart slamming into my ribcage.

Hidden by the tablecloth, Mateo moved his fingers across my thigh. I tried to stay quiet, but the pleasure of his hand had my leg stiffening under his caress. Carefully, I caught his hand, and moved it to my knee.

Taking a deep breath, I watched as the ghost of a smile played at the corners of his sensual mouth.

After dinner Mateo gave us a tour of Guadalajara, pointing out classic cathedrals and buildings from the colonial period of Spanish rule.

He took us up to a bluff that overlooked the valley. We all clamored out of the car and walked a broad path, giving us a panoramic view of the illuminated city.

When we got back to the hotel Janet embraced Mateo. "Thank you, Mateo, for a fabulous evening."

"I'm glad you enjoyed yourself. Raul is a Master Chef."

"The hotel pool is open. Why don't you two take advantage of it?"

"I didn't think to bring bathing trunks."

"I know the hotel provides bathing suits and towels for guests and visitors," Janet countered.

Mateo looked to me, seeking a clue to the appropriate response.

"Let's do it," I said, my eyes burning, "I'll go back to the room and find my bathing suit, if you want to get a suit from the desk clerk."

"Okay, I'll see you in ten minutes at the pool," he said staring brazenly back at me.

There were three grotto pools, aqua blue inside a glass enclosed pavilion. Hyacinths and ferns crowded together with twenty-foot-tall banana trees. A beautiful man-made world of plants and water.

I spotted him standing at the small bar set up near the deep end of the largest pool. His tan and chiseled physique caused me to catch a gasp in my throat as I approached him. Instinctively I pulled Janet's borrowed cover-up tight to my body. I bit my bottom lip and moved close to him, my arm bumping his casually.

"I ordered us Pellegrino."

"Great," I said, my Jell-O brain refusing to come up with anything more intelligent or amusing.

"Why don't you pick out a place for us to sit," he suggested as he balanced two Pellegrino bottles and two ice filled glasses on a small tray.

"I came to swim," I teased.

I looked down at my bare feet before gaining courage to look back up at him with open sexual abandon.

"And swim we shall," he said eyeing me closely. He obviously knew how he was affecting me. I couldn't escape the primal message his eyes were sending.

I wished there had been music to accompany the little dance I did, slowly taking off Janet's cover up, my tiny string bikini revealing a hell of a lot more than it covered up.

Before he could set the tray on the chosen table, I ran full throttle toward the water and dove in. As I came up for air, I saw him next to me and we came up together. His arms surrounded my waist and his mouth found mine, his tongue exploring and coaxing mine to respond.

The pool belonged to us and we claimed a space against the edge of a shadowed island toward the back of the grotto. The only light provided by colored stringers looped across the entire pool pavilion. In the half shadows, his body pressed into mine and his fingers explored my hair and face. Tender lips caressed my neck and chest.

27

My irreverent hand reached for the front of his bathing trunks and I watched his expression turn to molten lava. I paused momentarily, holding on to its firmness, our skin separated only by flimsy material.

He took an index finger and ran it gently across my bottom lip. My whole body shivered. I watched as rivulets of water slid down his chest, golden brown and gently heaving. My hand dropped, sliding slowly down his thigh. Eyes locked, entwined in the heaviness of sexual desire.

He broke the tension, bent down, and blew lightly on my ear lobe. A sweet sensation warmed my body, causing me to jerk rhythmically in pleasure.

"I won't do anything you are uncomfortable with," he whispered.

His look was intense. His tone earnest.

I looked up at him, warm with desire. My pussy heating up like an inferno between quivering thighs.

I pushed my face into his chest. My hand moved across his abdomen and he jerked involuntarily. I loved the firmness of his body and the softness of his skin. He smelled of soap, and musk.

I felt his hand cover mine and slowly intimately he guided my hand toward his erection and I once again took hold of the stiffened organ. Mateo moved his hips, causing my

28

hand to move up and down the shaft. I bit my lip and closed my eyes. All my nerves taut. Nervousness colliding with anticipation.

He moved my body slowly, pushing me gently to a shallow island under a dramatic and artfully created waterfall. In the shadows far from the bar, he boosted himself onto a rock shelf. I watched as he lowered his bathing trunks, exposing his manhood to me.

As I took his cock in my hand, Mateo placed his hand on the top of my head, using light pressure, he directed my head to his crotch.

I licked around the head of his shaft wetting it heavily with my saliva. He moved his hips, and his cock pushed its way into my open mouth.

He is large and I had to relax my throat to accommodate him. I moved up and down licking and sucking rhythmically, pushing him toward climax. As his sexual hunger intensified, he took a handful of my hair and used it to push my head up and down faster and more forcefully.

As his body stiffened, he groaned deeply. I prepared to swallow but Mateo was not a high school boy. He pulled away slowly easing himself from my mouth. He quickly joined me in the pool.

I wrapped my arms around him, pulling him close. He eagerly returned my embrace. Leaning into me he kissed me deeply and passionately. He took a handful of my hair and tugged on it pulling my head back. I felt tender bites traveling up and down my neck before he returned to my mouth.

Mateo reached behind me and pinched my ass. Once, and then again, and again. I groaned audibly as pain and pleasure slammed through me right to my groin.

He took my hips in both hands and pulled me solidly against him. The scent of sex was heavy in the air.

I felt his fingers tugging down my bikini bottoms.

I grabbed both of his hands, "I-I'm still a virgin," I stammered, "I'm not a tease. Please, please, don't be angry. I'm so sorry."

He slowly exhaled a breath and his respirations slowed. After a moment he kissed me sweetly, his hands moving to my face.

"You can trust me."

His arms surrounded me, and he rocked me like I was a tearful child, allowing us both time to cool down our sexual passion.

Why had I told him? Why had I stopped him?

I knew the answer. Fear. Fear of losing something long valued, something long cherished. I wished I had embraced my emerging womanhood, instead of holding on to childish innocence. It was too late, he saw me for what I was, a frightened child.

Chapter Four

Breaking News

The Mexican road block the previous summer had stuck with me. When Jimmy T. made up my documents, I had him make me a Texas nursing license along with a driver's license, passport, social security card, fishing license, and insurance card. I thought, "Medico" might give me a quick exit from most unwanted stops.

I bought a stethoscope, a blood pressure cuff, and a small First Aid kit with a big red cross on the top, just to sell the story. I liked the idea of being a nurse. Even a pretend nurse was appealing. I had planned on doing genetic research but being a faux nurse would have to do for now.

After a restless night and an agonized review of the maps, I decided Caracas was way too far to go. Even Costa Rica, by land was too far. There were miles of dangerous jungle to navigate with poor roads, and few to no roadside amenities. Not to mention the bad hombres just waiting for foolish travelers. I didn't want to do life in prison, nor did I want to end up a sex slave to a band of guerillas in Guatemala or Honduras.

Mexico was and still is a dangerous place, where drug lords and sex traffickers are so emboldened, they feel comfortable shooting up Mazatlán and other tourist enclaves.

Yet, Guatemala and Nicaragua can be even worse, especially for a girl alone on an unnamed jungle road. There's always a scarier monster.

Belize now made the most sense. For one thing, Belize borders Mexico to the south, so it is relatively close. It had been a British colony and English is spoken everywhere. Also, I had been there. Last year for two weeks on family vacation. I loved it. My Dad had even admitted the exchange rate was great.

I expected it would be a relatively safe place for a fugitive American teen to hang out for a while, that is if I could get across the Mexican-Belize border.

With the first glimmer of light, I filled my two ice chests with ice and grabbed a stack of bath towels, hand towels, and half a dozen wash cloths off an unattended maid cart.

I placed one of the ice chests on the passenger seat and secured it with the seat belt. The second chest I placed on the floor. I went back into the room and ran through my mental check list, making sure I hadn't left so much as a pair of panties.

Satisfied, I picked up a still damp towel from last night's shower and wiped down the entire room. I reassured myself my paranoia was justified because someone really was chasing me.

Just before getting behind the wheel I carefully arranged the stethoscope and blood pressure cuff, along with my First Aid kit in open view on the back seat.

I'm a fan of Film Noir and am acutely aware of the scenario in which a desperate fugitive is pulled over for a broken headlight, or a faulty turn signal.

As such I ran a complete system's check and kept my insurance and registration card within easy reach, remembering how Janet had handled Mateo.

I pulled out of the Little Alamo Motel parking lot, drove two blocks, and pulled into a Brookshire's Market. I bought some fruit and veggies, a six pack of Cokes, two flats of bottled water, and stocked the ice chests with my purchases. I also bought toilet paper and at least my sixth new burner phone.

In the parking lot, I looked again at the ragged and worn Rand McNally Atlas that had been my faithful companion since leaving Oregon. I refreshed my driving plan, and carefully edged into heavy morning traffic.

Half a mile from the Brookshire's I spotted the freeway entrance and pulled onto the ramp marked South to Brownsville and Matamoros, Mexico. I'd done this gig before. So, when I stopped at an insurance broker's office in Brownsville I was prepared.

34

I gave him $240 to cover the cost of fifteen days of Mexican auto insurance, and a visa. The insurance agent reminded me, he would need another $200 for an auto bond, which he told me would be returned when I exited Mexico. I grinned and gave a mental adios to my money. Such is the life of a fugitive.

The agent told me he couldn't do a currency exchange, but he pointed me to a small bank across the street.

The currency exchange was simple and speedy. I turned $1,500 American dollars into Mexican pesos. I knew I'd use the peso notes every time I stopped for gas or hit a toll road.

I convinced the bank manager to allow me to use the bank's restroom, claiming Crohn's disease. I didn't want to show much money in Mexico, or anywhere else for that matter. I kept six $20 peso notes in my billfold and distributed the remaining $20 peso notes between each of my red Chuck Taylor's and each bra cup. The remaining bills I put in a plastic bag and taped it to my lower abdomen under my panties.

At the car, I attached the import permit to the windshield, just below the rearview mirror. I retrieved a deodorant stick from my travel bag and spread a swath under each arm. I tossed the deodorant back into my bag and freshened my makeup.

Whoever thinks running for your life is fast or quick is under a misconception. Since leaving Lake Oswego, I have spent more time waiting than moving. I have been forced to embrace patience. My goal is to never look as if I'm in a hurry. My repeated mantra, "be cool, look cool."

The traffic lines leading to the border were moving slowly. As such my car windows had been cleaned three times for a cost of $3.00.

The Gateway International Bridge crosses the Rio Grande River. I paid the toll and when I looked up, I saw the port of entry sign welcoming travelers to Matamoros.

It was already one o'clock in the afternoon and although I didn't want to get caught driving after dark on some desolate Mexican highway, I decided I wanted to get out of Matamoros as fast as I could. Matamoros, unfortunately, is much like Brownsville, ugly, dusty, and polluted. Leaving it for almost anywhere, seemed like a good idea. Of course, as I have learned, sometimes staying where you are isn't necessarily a bad thing.

I knew that I would have good light until probably 6:00, so I decided to head south to Tampico. Tampico is just a couple miles inland from the Gulf of Mexico. By my estimation it was about 150 miles south of Matamoros. I figured I could be there by late afternoon.

From Tampico it was 587 miles to Corozal Town, Belize. The atlas suggested 20 hours to make the trip. Twenty hours? At that rate, my top speed would be about 30 miles per hour. That was a bit unnerving to think about. For a girl in a hurry that was definitely bad news.

I was only twenty miles outside of Matamoros when I encountered horrific road conditions. There were massive craters, not unlike what you would expect after a direct hit by a meteor shower. In addition to the potholes and craters there were places where the road narrowed perilously challenging any semblance of two-way traffic.

Once past Soto La Marina the road conditions improved. The beauty of the Sierra Tamaulipas mountain range embraced me. Vibrant reds, oranges and purples surrounded me. Dramatic vistas emerged with each turn in the road. The scenery was breathtaking. Rolling clouds raced toward me but disappeared when I rounded the next corner. I was awed by the beauty of the rugged landscape.

Although, I was unfamiliar with this section of Mexico, I had learned from previous trips to this country that when a road sign indicated a speed limit change or a warning of any sort, there was most assuredly a real obstacle, and it might be just feet beyond the caution sign.

Besides congested small towns where horse carts, unrestrained dogs, and pedestrian traffic mixed dangerously with cars and trucks, there was always the very real threat of topes, or sets of vibradores. If you are unfortunate enough to hit one of these speed bumps going too fast, they can literally tear your car apart. I would liken it to hitting a down staircase at sixty miles an hour.

On the outskirts of a small unnamed village, I saw a Pemex station and pulled in and had the state attendant fill my tank. A man wearing a soiled straw hat stuck his head in the window and shoved a box of Chicklets in my face. I told him, "no". Then with his other hand he pushed a bag of Katos at me.

I handed him a $20 peso note and he handed me two bags of the delightful Guatemalan nuts. He also sold me a box of black licorice. I paid a boy a peso to wash both the headlights and the taillights of the Sportage. I paid for the gas and was quickly back on the road. Everybody was just trying to make an honest peso.

I had barely gone a half mile from my Pemex stop when I was halted at a checkpoint. A short Federal agent with serious eyes and a well-fed belly approached my car and asked my destination.

"Undetermined."

He made no request for my documents, but rather walked up and down the side of my car thumping it lightly with his closed fist.

Another half-dozen uniformed officers, played cards in the shade of a cluster of olive trees next to a small cinder block building. None of them made a move.

I pulled a $20 peso note from my bra and said, "Senor, cola, café?" and extended the bill in his direction.

It was a bribe, but it was an exceedingly small one, and in Mexico it is viewed as perfectly acceptable.

He took the folded currency, smiled, and said, "Gracias, Senorita."

"Por favor, Senor, fotografia?" I said pointing to my phone.

He stood straight and tall, his prominent stomach pulled taut. After I snapped his picture, he visibly relaxed, and with a wave motioned me on.

I reached Tampico as a blood red sun was setting. I drove nervously through its congested streets, bouncing over topes searching for a place to spend the night.

The traffic volume was exceptionally heavy. The tight narrow streets were plugged with large trucks. Many of the trucks appeared dangerously neglected with missing headlights and bald tires. Honking cars squeezed perilously amongst the trucks and a flotilla of pedestrians and animal drawn carts jostled for position in the mass confusion. The streets had no dividing lines and half of the traffic signals were out of service.

Every intersection was a test of driver and pedestrian courage. Frustrated drivers played chicken with each other, challenging one another for the next turn at the crossings. Since making a left turn was a logistic nightmare, I proceeded forward hoping that I would miraculously find a motel by going straight ahead.

I had a sleeping bag and a two-man camp tent packed in the back of the SUV. I had hoped to maybe camp out along the way. The reality of sleeping amongst rattlesnakes and tarantulas quickly detoured those thoughts. Furthermore, a solitary car parked alone on a Mexican roadside is a magnet for trouble.

At last, I saw the lights of a small motel on the right side of the road surrounded by a courtyard wall, and I pulled my rig out of the traffic snarl and rented a room for the night.

The room was shabby but clean. There was a newer color TV and a lumpy queen bed with a faded blue bedspread. As with many hotels in Mexico there were no towels in the bathroom. You can always get towels, but you are charged for them. I was glad I had snagged the towels from the Little Alamo.

After a languid shower I opened the ice chest and made up a plate of fruit and veggies. I ate until I was full. It had been a long day. Now with a full belly I felt the exhaustion settle in. I laid down on the top of the bedspread, not intending to fall asleep.

It was just after midnight when I was awakened by the sound of two men yelling and cursing outside my room. The roughness of the language and the volume rapidly intensified. I found myself concerned that the situation might lead to gunfire. I gingerly pulled aside the corner of the too often washed curtain just far enough to see.

I couldn't afford to become involved in an event that drew a truck load of cops to the scene. The men squared-off ready to settle the matter physically. I didn't see any guns, but it looked like both had knives. If cursing were a deadly weapon both these guys would already be dead.

Suddenly, the motel office lights flashed on-and-off. I guess it was designed to get the attention of the combatants. I know it got my attention. A man's voice from the direction of the office bellowed in vulgar Spanish, "Cut the bullshit. The cops are on the way."

The would-be warriors exchanged an additional series of insults before breaking their adversarial stance. Their separate vehicles burning rubber as they roared from the parking lot.

Once the parking lot war ended, all went quiet. Wide awake, I turned on the television. A Mexican version of John

Walsh's *'America's Most Wanted'* started. The story focused on me. Unsure how much longer my trembling legs would hold me up, I dropped heavily into a nearby lounge chair.

A handsome well-known Mexican television personality was the face of the south of the border version of Walsh's crime show. *'North America's Most Wanted'* featured real crime tales from Mexico, Canada, and the United States. The angle was the usual with a Mexican twist, focusing primarily on drug lords, sex trafficking, gun smuggling, and border crimes.

"Tonight, we are going to feature Sky Evenson. Evenson is extremely dangerous. She may look young and beautiful, but she is suspected of two murders in Oregon and a multitude of resulting felonies."

I listened as the host continued, "Evenson is fluent in English, French and Spanish. She is comfortable with guns. She is the worst of the worst. We need to get this ruthless killer off the streets tonight and we are asking for your help. If you know the whereabouts of Sky Evenson we are asking you to make the call. You make the call, and we make the capture. Your tips have put over ninety dangerous criminals behind bars this year alone. Make that call!"

As usual, the program featured two criminal profiles during the thirty-minute show. I was sharing the episode with a Vietnamese enforcer responsible for half a dozen killings in a multi-state murder spree.

I had gotten used to the typical two, or three, minute news bulletins. The switch in coverage catapulted my fragile mental state to a condition of near madness.

Toward the end of the show the host pointed to a dozen sketches. Each depiction suggesting potential changes that I could have made to alter my appearance. A couple of them were alarmingly close to my adopted persona. A new look was obviously on the horizon.

At the end of the *'North America's Most Wanted'* presentation there was an update bulletin. In near breathless commentary, the reporter brought the viewing community up to speed on breaking news out of the United States. The commentator described the discovery of two bodies in a single shallow grave outside of Lindale, Indiana.

I was hyperventilating and consequently a bit lightheaded. I opened a bottle of water and tried to regain my equilibrium. Just trying to hold it together.

Several minutes of video crime scene footage took over the reporting. I watched, as no less than two dozen police cars, coroner rigs and forensic vehicles were pictured jamming a rural road, spilling over onto a grassy field, adjacent to a run-down farmhouse, and its surrounding cadre of ramshackle outbuildings.

I watched as men in white coveralls with CORONER emblazoned on their backs, carried two sealed body bags to a waiting white transfer van.

The Mexican reporter's audio came back on. His agitated commentary described a grizzly scene, telling viewers that the single shallow grave had been discovered less than twenty feet from the abandoned farmhouse, when equipment began prepping for a planned subdivision.

Leaked information suggested the bodies were discovered within hours of their burial. The short time between death and discovery of the bodies had facilitated the near immediate, forensic identification of Cory Davis and Ward Haskins.

The news alert switched suddenly to a hastily arranged Portland, Oregon press conference. Kate Snyder, the head of the Portland FBI office briefed reporters.

"The search for Sky Evenson has now shifted to the Indianapolis, Indiana area and is classified as an utmost priority. We believe her to be extremely dangerous."

After Snyder finished her update the next person to come to the lectern to address the gathered crowd of reporters was Congressman Jerry Johnson. Jerry Johnson's involvement in the case had stimulated intense public interest in the manhunt. Droves of cameramen and reporters clamored around the stage. It wasn't every day that one of the most powerful men in the country got involved in a case of murder and suspected cyber-espionage.

Johnson was perfectly groomed in a dark grey suit, and burgundy tie. Jerry was the carefully crafted, and curried image, of a high-powered American politician. He coughed to clear his throat before he spoke.

Johnson read from a prepared statement "on behalf of my dead wife and myself, I want to thank all those involved in the recovery of my beloved stepson's body. There is a lot more to this story and we will be doing everything possible to bring Cory and Ward's killer to justice.

I was glad Cory was beyond hearing the congressman's professional-grade misinformation campaign. Bullshit, pure bullshit. Cory had detested his stepfather. He would often go through the congressman's private files and even his shirt and coat pockets looking for anything juicy. Anything he might use to convince his mother to divorce Johnson.

Lloyd Haskins, Ward's Dad, a high priced and well-respected Portland attorney, was up next to the lectern. Mr. Haskins was measured in tone. Very much the professional. Speaking to the crowd he said it was important to "respect the process," and "not race to judgment."

My parents were last to the podium. Red-eyed and defeated, they held hands as they approached the

45

microphones. My Dad blew his nose into a handkerchief before trying to raise the microphone to a more comfortable height.

The second big celebrity draw to the Portland, Oregon press conference was my Father. Cal "The Spark" Evenson is a 6'11" NBA superstar. My Daddy has spent the last 12 years of his legendary career as star forward for the Portland Trailblazers. After a moment or two of frustration he managed to adjust the microphone to a more favorable position for him to talk.

Still holding my Mother's hand, sunken eyed and haggard, Daddy looked straight into the camera. He cleared his throat.

"Sky, if you can hear me and you are able to do it, please, call the FBI and turn yourself in. We will get this whole thing straightened out. We love you."

I slid off the chair onto the floor and sobbed. No matter how much I wanted to shut it off, I needed to hear every detail of the reporting.

The reporting broke away from the Portland feed and went back to WTTV Indianapolis. The anchor was reporting that there were unsubstantiated but credible and extremely disturbing reports out of the Coroner's Office that indicated Davis and Haskins had undergone extreme torture and mutilation, before being shot in the back of the head.

"Torture and mutilation."

I tried to absorb what that meant. Cory Davis was in great physical shape. He was Oregon HS State Heavyweight Wrestling Champion, for crying out loud. Two years in a row. He biked 5-10 miles every day.

Ward was also in amazing shape. He was a fabulous skier, hiker, runner, and sailor. He had the body of a god. Michele Morrone comes to mind. I just couldn't imagine the two of them being overpowered. The likely scenario included weapons and multiple assailants.

Not only are Ward and Cory both dead, but they were tortured and mutilated. How could I possibly end up the prime suspect in such a crime? Women aren't well-known for mutilating people. Before, or after death. That's usually more of a man thing. Where the hell is the FBI profiler? There is no way a profiler in their right mind would sign off on the theory that had Sky Evenson as the killer of Cory Davis and Ward Haskins.

The reporter continued, indicating that high ranking authorities believed that Sky Evenson might still be in the Indianapolis area. Authorities were sounding alarm bells that went beyond the FBI's 10 Most Wanted List. The commentator confirmed I had just been placed on Interpol's Most Wanted International Criminals List.

Authorities believed I had become a threat to anyone who might be unlucky enough to encounter me. Most authorities interviewed voiced the belief that I was headed to Mexico, probably through Texas. Or, to Eastern Canada through Michigan.

The FBI reward was up to $150,000. The families of Ward and Cory added an additional $150,000 for a total of $300,000.

I headed to the bathroom and puked until I began retching, dry heaves doubling me over. The irony of their lies was not lost on me, but what were they doing in Indiana together?

Why had they been buried together in the same grave? That kind of crap is just, wrong. Sick. If you are going to kill someone either leave them where they fall or take some time and dig everybody a grave.

What the hell I thought, is there no respect for the dead? But, even more than all of that, how could I be implicated in their murders? I was 2,000 miles from Indiana. I collapsed on the bed and cried until I could cry no more.

It was becoming more obvious to me, that I probably would never make it to the courtroom.   If the bad guys had found Cory and Ward, how much longer would it be before they found me? If they found Jimmy T. they would learn about my forged documents. More importantly, they would find out the name I was using.

Every muscle and fiber in my body tensed to its limit. I sat crippled in that Tampico motel room and prayed for the first time in an exceptionally long time.

Jimmy was my primary concern. Would he claim the $300,000 reward money? For some reason I doubted it. Unless of course he was arrested on another charge and needed a plea bargain. Then again, I knew next to nothing about human behavior. It was more likely he would run for the border himself, fearing that he might be considered an accomplice to a growing string of murders. I think Jimmy T. had as many secrets as I did. I suspected he would continue to cling to the shadows.

After the tears, came bone chilling terror. Fear and anxiety kept me pacing the room most of the night. It wasn't until four in the morning that I found escape in sleep.

I opened my eyes to the maid tapping on the door. I opened the door several inches and shaded my eyes to bright sunshine.

"I'll be out in 15 minutes."

I scrambled about the room gathering my few belongings together before I washed my face and put on a clean blouse and a fresh pair of shorts.

I wiped down the room with a damp towel and loaded my personal effects into the Sportage. I had the maid bring me two buckets of ice for my coolers and handed her a $20 peso note for her trouble. It was not enough to cause her to remember me, but enough to thank her for her assistance.

Wearing sunglasses and a baseball cap I scanned the perimeter before getting behind the wheel of the little SUV. I had a pounding headache. My hands shook violently against the steering wheel and my right eye quivered with a nervous tic.

I pulled a bottle of Coke from the ice chest and took several large gulps, before dumping four Tylenol gel caps into my hand and propelling them down my throat with a jerk of my head. I followed the capsules with two more swallows of Coke before I started my rig.

I knew I couldn't continue this insanity for much longer. I had only one choice and that choice was six hundred miles in the opposite direction.

After seeing the previous night's television report, I knew the cops, the Speaker's associates, the FBI, the Mexican Federales, and at least half the population of both nations had been agitated by the increased reward and heavy media exposure to track me down. $300,000 was a considerable motivator. I could almost see the pitchforks and torches.

As I chewed on an apple I thought through my evolving situation. I had been out of the United States for less than 36 hours. I knew this breaking news story posed a perilous problem. When big money is combined with intense media coverage the populace springs to life and things begin to happen, which is usually bad news for the fugitive in the spotlight.

I was convinced that my best chance at survival was back in the U.S. Getting back across the border was fraught with danger. But staying in Mexico likely meant a Mexican jail, repeated rapes, and merciless beatings. Going back to the U.S. was like every other recent decision, circumstances had already made the choice for me. I didn't dare get stuck south of the border with its endless roadblocks, stops, and searches.

I nervously navigated the congested streets of Tampico looking for an exit highway. I turned on the air conditioning and the cool air helped a little. I lifted the lid of the ice chest and pulled out a chilled bottle of water and rubbed the cold plastic across my cheeks, neck, and forehead. I made my way through the narrow streets until I saw a solitary sign and turned.

Chapter Five

Contact

I drove into bright sunshine, but within an hour storm clouds rolled in from the coast, bringing a heavy downpour. I rolled up the car windows and turned my wiper blades to high. Although heavy, the rainstorm was short lived, and within half an hour the clouds broke over the mountains and the sun snuck out, casting a pink glow over the landscape.

I couldn't get the image of my father and mother's red-eyed and ashen faces out of my head. I never wanted to hurt my parents. What must they think? Seeing their pain broke my heart.

Traffic was non-existent. I hadn't seen a car or another human being for at least 30 minutes. I was on the verge of tears, with a complete breakdown imminent. I pulled the car off the road. I opened the vehicle door and climbed out. Despite my fear of rattlesnakes and tarantulas, I took a brief walk along the roadside, trying to steady my nerves.

Maybe I should call home, at least tell my parents I was alive and safe for the moment. Of course, that was impossible. The FBI was surely monitoring all my family's phones. They could have a GPS drone pinpoint me in minutes.

I stood alone in a foreign land 2,700 miles from home, without a clue as what to do next. I felt a wave of terror wash over me. I took several deep breaths, forcing my heart rate into submission. I reminded myself of my mantra, 'be cool, look cool.'

I opened the door and clung to it. I willed my failing body through the open portal. Behind the wheel once again I grasped it for reassurance, and sat eyes glued shut, using it as an anchor to stop the earth from drifting out of orbit.

I managed to pull a cup of pomegranate seeds from the cooler and popped the plastic top and took a sip from a bottled water and spilled a mouthful of the sweet seeds into my mouth.

"What the fuck," I mumbled to myself stupidly, still sucking on pomegranate seeds and sifting through all the useless crap in my purse, "I have it, I know it's here."

According to all the crime shows, phone tracking is one of the easiest ways for cops to catch fugitives. Knowing that common police tactic, I had left my family cell phone in my RX7 when I left it in a Tacoma parking lot back in June. But before I did, I'd taken time to write down all the phone numbers on my contact list.

I found the burner phone from Brookshire's and called a number written on a page of my little phone book.

As the rings continued, fear again seized me, and I was about to disconnect when I heard a soft, "Hello."

"I-I-I, shouldn't have called."

There was a palpable silence, broken by soft breathing, on the other end of the line.

"Don't talk unless I ask a question."

I guess I shouldn't have been surprised. I'm on the 24-hour news shows, 24 hours a day.

"Are you here?"

"Twelve hours away."

"Tonight, or tomorrow?"

"Tomorrow."

I heard the line go silent and I tossed the burner phone back in my purse. Taking another sip of water, I finished the pomegranate snack. Done, I dropped the plastic cup into my makeshift trash bag.

My plan was to find a room early this evening and hang out until tomorrow afternoon before finishing the last leg of the trip. The last thing I wanted to do was arrive frazzled, disheveled, and looking desperate.

Twelve hours was far more time than I probably needed, ten hours was a better estimate, but my familiarity with the Mexican road system gave me cause to doubt a swift trip.

After a good night's sleep, I woke up feeling better than I had in months. The weather was pleasant as I got ready to leave the Leon Student Hostel. I had been the only guest. The host seemed delighted to have me stay into the late afternoon and we shared a coffee on the rooftop patio.

His name was Miguel Trujillo. He was young, with happy eyes and friendly demeanor. He wanted to show me the catacombs, the art museum and several of the city's classic cathedrals. He was sweet and a bit lonely I could tell.

We spoke comfortably and naturally, like old friends. I thanked him for the tour offer, but explained I was on my way to meet my Aunt Janet in Guadalajara.

Miguel gave me detailed instructions on how to find Highway 80 from the hostel. It was a decent road and would provide me a straight shot to Guadalajara. He said it should be an easy drive.

Miguel helped me load my baggage. We hugged naturally and spontaneously as I pulled out my keys getting ready to depart. I prayed this wasn't as bad a change of direction as my worried brain was predicting. As I turned on the ignition, I felt an uneasiness settle over me.

The drive was uneventful. When I got to the outskirts of Guadalajara, I pulled off the road. I retrieved the burner phone from the bottom of my purse, sucked in a gulp of air and pressed redial.

"Got a pen and paper?"

"Yes," I answered.

"Stay on Highway 80. It will take you through Guadalajara. As you get toward the northerly end of town the road will change to Highway 23. Then without notice it becomes Highway 15. At the little village of La Venta del Astillero you will see signs to Nextipac. There will be a Pemex station at that corner. Make a right turn and follow the road toward Nextipac. In 3.2 miles you will see a high adobe wall on the left side of the road. Drive until you see an open gate. Turn in. Close the gate behind you. Drive up to the house, about ½ mile up the hill. Don't come before 7:00 tonight. Understand?"

"Yes," I croaked.

Once again, I was left alone with a dial tone.

Daylight was quickly vanishing when I turned off the highway at 7:15. After pulling onto the property, I stopped in the middle of the road, got out of the Sportage, and closed the gate behind me as I had been instructed. I climbed back into my rig and headed down the road. I could see up on a cliffside a low-slung house silhouetted against a setting sun.

The little SUV clung to the road as it climbed up the hillside, finally depositing me in front of a large and beautifully landscaped glass and adobe home. I checked my face in the visor mirror, and decided it was as good as it was going to get. I held my position, trying to convince my legs to move.

The driver's side door opened, leaving me exposed and vulnerable.

"Bienvenida. Mi casa es tu casa."

"Mateo. I'm so sorry. I don't want to cause you any problems."

I slid from behind the wheel and stood in front of him. I was poised to throw my arms around him, but unsure, his demeanor unreadable. I stood waiting. He answered my concern by initiating a tender embrace.

"I never would have recognized you," followed quickly with, "Let's get you inside."

He took my hand and led me across a beautiful front patio and into the house.

"What an incredible house."

"Luis Barragan. One of his early masterpieces from 1980."

"It seems to belong to the earth and the sky."

"Yes, it is the endless use of glass and the expansive rooms. It was commissioned by an American actor, Rock Hudson. I understand he came here only twice. Apparently he died of AIDS."

"I've never heard of him."

"I had never heard of him either until the real estate agent gave me a bit of history. But together he and Barragan created a timeless classic."

Mateo gave me a tour. The master suite was the size of a soccer field, with a bathroom befitting Julius Caesar. The kitchen was 21st century. He told me he had spent two months with a crew of ten carpenters and 6 stone masons cleaning and refurbishing the house before he could move in.

Apparently, the house had been vacant for nearly thirty years. Tied up in lawsuits, estate issues, and heavy tax liens. During that time, the house had become home to snakes, bats, armadillos, and prairie dogs.

At last, he showed me to a light and spacious guest room at the back of the house. It had a private bath and a sliding door to a small patio with a waterfall feature and a hot tub. The lights of Guadalajara shone in the distance.

"This room will be yours. Will it work?"

"Yes. It's beautiful. Thank you."

"If you want to freshen up, I'll unload your car.

"I do need to use the restroom. Thank you."

When I came out of the bathroom Mateo was carefully placing my clothes in the drawers of a large armoire and hanging those things that needed to be hung up in the large walk-in closet.

"I'm not staying," I said awkwardly.

"Yes, you are. For a while at least. You need to rest. You need to make some major decisions," he paused and looked at me for several seconds before he said, "Most importantly, you need to be held and hugged."

"I called you because I hoped you could help me. So much has happened. I haven't been able to stop running."

He put his arm around my shoulder and gave me one of his knee-buckling smiles, "I'm all yours. I've taken two weeks off."

"Really?"

"Really."

I felt a deep sigh of relief.

"I've fixed up a couple of steaks. Let's eat."

"I don't think I can eat," I said looking at my feet.

"You can eat. There's homemade vanilla ice cream for dessert."

"That sounds like a bribe."

"Maybe. Anyway, let's eat. I've set up everything out by the pool."

After dinner we sat on the patio and I brought up my predicament.

"Do you think you can help me get out of Mexico?" I asked knowing I was asking the near impossible.

There was a long and heavy silence, before he spoke.

"You know I'm a cop. You are asking me to implicate myself in at least a dozen felonies. Your being here could end my career and send me to prison for a decade. Jesus."

"P-p-please, Mateo, don't be angry. I swear to you, I didn't kill anybody."

"I hope not," his voice cold and brittle, "because if you are lying to me," his eyes imprisoning mine, "I will personally see to it that you spend the next fifty years in prison. Do you understand me?"

"So much has happened. I understand now we should never have run, but we were terrified."

"Let's save this until tomorrow. I need to go to bed. I've been pulling double shifts for the last two months because of a big sex trafficking case I'm heading. I want you to get some sleep but be up early, I want to go sailing tomorrow. I have a boat moored on Lake Chapala."

"Okay," I said weakly.

He stood and excused himself. No kiss, no hug, just a soft, "Good night."

Chapter Six

Captured

The morning found me sitting between two other convicts, shackles at my wrists and ankles. I had a big ass headache.

The one on my right was having a conversation with an unseen person, and as such made no fucking sense. She was apparently off her meds. The one on my left hadn't said a word since we loaded up. My gut told me I should be glad for that.

A Jalisco State officer opened the back of the cargo van and a U.S. agent looked in. I kept my eyes directed down, boring a hole in the van's floorboard, doing my best impression of a non-entity.

The girl on my right kept up her one-way conversation as the stony silence to the left persisted. The silent one, meditating on a tiny black spot on the van's interior wall.

The U.S. agent looked at each of us in turn, flipping through the official transfer documents, "Murder to general mayhem. Hell, this one looks like a concentration camp victim," turning back to the Captain for an explanation.

"She didn't like our accommodations," he said with no sense of amusement in his voice, "she's spent the last three weeks on some crazy ass hunger strike."

"And this one? She looks catatonic," pointing to the 'quiet one,' "You got her on some kind a psych restraint?"

"Absolutely not! Murder One. The warrant states she shot her lover twice in the back of the head while he slept."

"Hmm," was the U.S. Marshall's only comment.

Mateo continued, "I've never understood domestic abuse murders. I understand there is a psych component to it but, I don't understand why these women can't just get in the car and leave."

I kept my eyes hooded and my mouth shut.

"I wouldn't know," the U.S. agent deadpanned, "what's the story on this one?" pointing to chatterbox.

"Apparently she's having a psychotic break. She was arrested after breaking into a pastry shop. When the boys found her, she was sitting on the floor stuffing her face with capirotada and churro and talking to the Almighty."

"Looks like a bus full of crazies. My first inclination is to send you and your lady friends here back south. But I guess since they came from here, I've got to take them."

63

He signed Mateo's paperwork with a quick scribble. He expelled an audible sigh before handing the clipboard back to Mateo.

The door to the van slammed shut and I recognized Mateo's voice saying to the Jalisco officers, "I'll meet you guys at the Court House. I'm riding with Jose. Keep the prisoner's in the van until I get there. Understood?"

"Yes, Captain Rios," came the response twice fold.

I stared at my knotted fingers. My heart was pounding like a jackhammer. Sweat trickled down my face. I hunched my shoulders trying to minimize my existence, imagining myself the size of an atom. My brain was crowded with crazy thoughts spiraling like a kaleidoscope, first one direction and then another, crashing into each other at the speed of a particle accelerator.

I was without a doubt on the rain-slicked precipice of a panic attack. Screaming on the inside like an Edvard Munch masterpiece.

I could hear the Mexican cops chattering comfortably between themselves while I was whipped down the chamber of my own Hadron collider, smashing through quarks and electrons seeking the answer to anti-matter.

In less than ten minutes the van came to a stop.

"We're returning three of your finest," the Mexican officer laughs. "Captain Rios has the paperwork. He went ahead to the Court House."

The voice from outside our rig said sternly, "All prisoners transferred from Mexico now need to go up to the Judicial Clerk's Office at the Court House. We no longer take custody of prisoners until they have been seen by a Federal judge. They now review all paperwork up there for correctness and then each prisoner must appear in front of a Federal Court judge within 4 hours of hitting U.S. soil.

"When did all this start?" one of the Jalisco officers asked.

The American officer countered, "Last month."

"So, what happened?"

"We had a few minor screw ups around here, and suddenly everyone's got their panties in a knot."

"Like what?"

"There were a couple civil rights lawsuits. The Feds got involved and suddenly the DOJ was telling us how to do things. So, to tamp things down, we agreed to change a few procedures."

"And what does that mean to us?"

"What that means for you 'ol buddy, is you need to turn this rig around, head downtown and find one of those spaces reserved for "Official Vehicles" across the street from the Federal Court House and take your business inside."

There was a short pause before I heard, "Okay. Thanks, man."

Apparently, we were going back to where we had just come from. The trip downtown took about ten minutes. It was the longest ten minutes of my life. As the van came to a halt, I thought my heart would too.

The van door opened, and Mateo, flanked by three Jalisco State cops, looked in at their sweating cargo.

"Bienvenida a los estados unidos!"one smart ass said.

The cadre of Mexican officers led by Mateo, were quickly reinforced by half a dozen U.S. Marshalls. Shackled together we awkwardly disembarked the van. Each of us carried a large grocery sack filled with hygiene supplies and the clothes we were wearing when we were arrested.

We struggled awkwardly up the steps of the Federal Courthouse. Once inside, we were ushered to a holding area where the chain linking us together was removed. We were then directed to sit on one of a series of long wooden benches.

The crazy one was up first. The first step in the process took her up to a glass enclosure separating, and essentially securing several office workers, from the prisoner's holding tank.

I looked through downcast lashes and saw a wafer-thin clerk shuffle a stack of papers. Every other page she would ask a question her horn rimmed glasses riding near the end of her nose.

It was like clockwork. The steady beat as the clerk stamped each page in the crazy one's packet of papers. She then picked up the phone, talked on it for less than a minute, handed the paperwork to the U.S. Marshall, who led the prisoner through a door marked Hearing Room.

The silent one was next. It all played out again. Like a song stuck on replay. Every detail just the same as the first time around. The dehumanizing effect of bureaucracy.

Mateo stood over me, flanked by a burly young U.S. Marshall. The Marshall nodded me in the direction of the partition. I was stiff after so many hours riding in the van. I rose slowly clinging to my life crammed into a recycled grocery bag.

My body fought my brain every inch of the way as I did as I was told. The walk from the bench to the interrogation booth both the shortest and the longest distance in the world. Everything in me screaming it was the first stop before the execution chamber.

The clerk was younger than I thought, distance altering my perspective. Much younger, and much prettier. She relieved Mateo of the offered document package and gave him a sultry look before giving me a quick up and down assessment.

Pushing her wayward glasses back in place, she read through my documents with the efficiency of a civil servant. There was none of her usual questioning and I watched as a weary frown froze itself in place.

"Captain Rios, I am sorry to say I am truly disappointed."

She brought her two hands together, resting them motionless on top of the pile of paperwork.

"Your paperwork is usually exemplary. However, what I have here appears to be false incarceration. I'm going to run her prints for U.S. wants and warrants. If she comes up clean, I'm going to throw your paperwork in the trash and release her immediately."

Mateo lowered his head as she continued, dropping her voice, so only those closest to her could hear, concluding coldly, "This kind of bullshit. This kind of sloppy paperwork is exactly why we've had to change the way we do things around here. Do you know anything about 'unlawful detainment'? 'false imprisonment?'"

Mateo was silent. A paragon of silent stoicism. I wasn't sure about him, but I was wondering could I get to the door before the bullets caught up with me. Silly fantasy.

"In this country it's kind of a big deal," the clerk added.

Mateo sacrificed himself to her outrage, spending time studying his shoes

"Your office was advised weeks ago, of the new prisoner transfer requirements. Don't ever allow this to happen again, or we'll be going up the food chain, if you get my meaning."

All sex and sultry glances had disappeared, leaving only cold distain and severe reprimand.

The bulky U.S. Marshall's face was impassive, no sign of support or disapproval. He must be a hell of a poker player, I thought.

Mateo looked up from his surveillance of his highly shined uniform boots and said, "We'll sit over there. You'll give me a heads up when the 'wants and warrants' results come back?" he asked.

"Yes," the clerk replied coldly.

He sat next to me and waited. The clock in the holding area was just moving to 11:21 when Mateo was beckoned back to the glass window. I couldn't hear what she said, but the change was clear. Although still obviously miffed she was once again casting those sultry eyes in his direction.

The authorities stateside had my image. Many versions in fact. I didn't think they had my prints though. One of the advantages of never having been arrested. Of course, the FBI could have pulled them from any of my personal items at my parent's house.

Mateo motioned for one of the Jalisco State officers to release me.

"Take your bag, go into the Ladies Room across the hall and change your clothes. Bring the jumpsuit back to me. You've got 5 minutes."

"Yes, of course. Thank you," I said, intending to throw up my guts first.

I held my head over the sink, but nothing came up but a retching sound. My head screamed and my hands shook like an alcoholic in withdrawal.

Quickly rinsing my mouth, I pulled on my white baggy shorts and a very tight black T-shirt. I took the big lash mascara wand from the grocery bag and layered on the black paint as thick as I could manage. Satisfied, I pulled on my pink ball cap and slipped on my Ray Bans.

I gathered the prison jumpsuit from the floor and nearly ran out into the hall, anxious to rid myself of the convict garb.

Mateo was standing in a circle with the other Mexican cops when I extended my arm with the garment dangling from my hand. He motioned for one of the other officers to take it from me.

I was about to walk toward the exit when his voice halted me, "Por favor, Senorita. I will need you to sign some paperwork."

"Okay," I said, not having anything else to say.

Turning back to his fellow officers he pulled his billfold from his back pocket and said, "Here take this," handing several bills to each of the officers, "Dinner is on me. Keep your receipts and I'll sign a voucher when I get back to the office. You boys shift each other behind the wheel. I want you driving straight through, pee stops, fill ups and meals excluded of course. I'll turn over the stolen vehicle to Webb County Sheriff's Department. I have several personal matters to take care of here and I'll fly out tomorrow morning. Any questions?"

When none of the officers offered any questions Mateo continued, "Okay then, who's got the keys to the Sportage?"

I heard the jingle of my car keys; and saw them fly past my head. Mateo caught them easily with a raised hand.

He adjourned the impromptu meeting, sharing handshakes all around with his team. They disbanded informally and headed for the nearest green exit sign. When the last of the three men exited the building, Mateo turned to me.

"Your clearance documents," Mateo said, handing me an oversized manilla envelope, "Walk with me, please."

Mateo halted at the top of the courthouse steps,

"I forgot to ask where they parked your rig," he laughed.

I laughed with him, as usual, unable to grow an intelligent comment in the dust bowl of my brain. Something that only happened when I stood close to him.

He hit the key fob and we saw the lights and heard the horn of the Sportage. It was parked in an "Official Vehicles Only" lot across the street from where we stood.

"We've got some unfinished business," he said huskily.

Chapter Seven

Motel Life

He closed the door behind us and pulled the drapery cord, closing out the daylight.

"They didn't get my prints, did they?"

"No."

"Whose fingerprints did you use?" I asked, turning to face him.

"My 96-year-old Aunt Maria's," he said solemnly.

I worried that he might now be questioning his actions, his mood visibly pensive.

"And my car?"

"I'm a sworn law enforcement officer. If I say a vehicle was reported stolen and there's a request for its return, I write up the paperwork and start the ball rolling. And if I happen to want to deliver the rig, I can assign myself to perform that task. Call it efficient police work."

"Okay, when they ran my Texas driver's license why didn't it show up as counterfeit?" I asked, searching his face.

"For your information," he said with a don't underestimate me kind of look, "You have a totally legal Mexican driver's license. I issued it myself, using the photo from your Texas license. Of course, I kept your Texas ID. I figured you might want them both."

I hugged him spontaneously, breathing in his sexy scent.

"Thank you for every minute of the last two weeks. Whatever the future brings I want you to know I have never been so happy. Hopefully, this nightmare called my life can get back on track. You have rekindled my hope. And today, of course, you gave me my freedom. Thank you."

I squeezed him tighter before hesitantly whispering, "I love you."

He returned the embrace, rubbing his hands up and down my back slowly, rhythmically. He reached out and found his phone. Soon sounds of soft rock filled the space.

I watched him, barely able to control my breathing. The room was shrinking around us, pushing us closer and closer together. He kissed behind my ear, my cheek and then my mouth, his tongue teasing and playing with mine.

"I want to make love to you."

"Yes," I replied without hesitation.

We stood there while the heat of our bodies threatened to spontaneously combust, neither of us moving out of range from the promised pyrotechnics.

"Take your clothes off."

He said it in such a flat matter-of-fact tone that I nearly missed it.

He locked the door and took several steps forward, "I think instead," with his eyes burning into me, "I'll do it for you."

Suddenly the outside world dissolved into the here and now. I felt his fingers lightly dragging down my cheek, followed by petal soft kisses.

We locked mouths our tongues joined in excited hunger. He pushed his body against me, causing me to fall easily into the nearby wall, pressing me firmly against its immovable surface.

I sent my fingers exploring his dark hair, weaving the strands between my fingers. Our mouths separated and he took a nip at my earlobe, sending jolts of electric current across my body. His tongue seeks the earlobe and licks the spot he had just bitten.

"Raise your arms over your head."

I did as I was told. Mateo continued to watch me closely. He pulled my T-shirt over my head, leaving my lace bra exposed, my nipples rigid, visibly pushing against the delicate material. I flushed slightly, while trying to rearrange my mussed hair with nervous fingers.

He untied the string waistband of my shorts and they drop, forming a crumpled wreath at my ankles. He heaves, his chest raising noticeably. I gulped audibly, trying desperately to fill my oxygen deprived lungs. His eyes burned, their intensity holding my lungs hostage, barely allowing me to suck in a breath.

He spun me around with the hand of an experienced policeman and ordered me to put my hands over my head.

He then began a gentle search of my hair and neck. He moved down my body searching my bra for contraband, finding only my sensitive breasts.

With a single move of his hand, my bra hooks yielded. Mateo took his time, moving each strap across each shoulder, allowing the binding to drop to the carpet.

He filled each hand with a breast, swirling his tongue around each nipple, before sucking each one in turn.

"You are perfect," he whispered.

He ran his hands up and down my back, my sides, and my stomach before I felt his fingers on each hip, inside my panties, pulling them down until I was naked.

The slow body cavity search began, his fingers searching my slit for moisture caused me to moan. He spent way too much time rubbing his other hand across my ass looking for something he just couldn't seem to find.

I wasn't sure what I was supposed to do. When he turned to face me, I was within inches of him. I reached out, and slowly began to unbutton his shirt. He blew out a breath of air, and I felt his body tense.

When I unfastened the final button of his uniform shirt, I took my time and removed each sleeve over each shoulder and down each arm before the garment dropped freely to the floor.

"Raise your hands over your head," I said, my tongue caressing his ear.

His eyes glistened. Eager to play, he obediently raised both arms above his head. I slowly began rolling his T-shirt from the bottom to the top. My hair brushed his belly, and my lips caught his nipples, each in their turn. I felt his gasp as I reached out and unhooked the top button of his uniform pants, my breath now teasing the hair just above his waistband. He arched his back as I painstakingly moved the zipper slowly down.

"Take your shirt off," I said quietly.

My voice was as sexy and throaty as I could manage, my actions dictated by movie scenes.

He pulled his white T-shirt over his head, as I bent over to untie his black government-issue boots, tossing each one in the corner with a clomp, followed by his socks.

He watched me through half closed lids, his breathing rate increasing. I stood back up, hooked my thumbs in the waist band of his underwear and slid them down, carefully accommodating his enormous erection, all the way to his ankles, where he stepped free of them.

"Let's get a shower," he said, "I feel like I've spent the afternoon being dragged back and forth across the floor of a Tijuana whorehouse."

I laughed and followed him.

He pushed aside the white plastic shower curtain, turned on the taps and stood testing the water.

He took my hand and led me into the tiny motel shower.

I squirted soap into my palms and rubbed them together before reaching for his engorged penis. Taking his cock in my hand, I grasped it firmly, listening for the change in his breathing.

78

Sliding my hands lower and lower I gently take his balls into my cupped hands. I massage them and tease them with loving fingers. My hand strays behind his balls and I rub the perineum slowly and tenderly and feel the rim of his anus tighten.

I lathered my hands and applied friction up and down his length, slowly and deliberately increasing pressure and speed. I watched his eyes smolder hot, his back arch, and his legs tense.

He reached down covering my hand with his.

"Stop, or I'm gonna' shoot my load," he said with a tortured grimace.

I soaped his body, and he returned the favor, soaping and teasing me to the brink of ecstasy before I say, "Stop, or I'm going to cum all over your hand," doing my best to mimic his earlier painful grimace, as I turn off the shower.

He took two towels from the rack. He wrapped one around me like a cocoon. He held me tight, my back now facing him. The second one he wrapped around his waist and hitched it.

"You're so damn beautiful."

Truthfully, only my parents had ever told me I was beautiful and certainly never "damn" beautiful. I was afraid to move, thinking I might break the spell. I was so afraid of loving him. It wasn't like there was going to be a future of white picket fences and adorable kids.

He turned me around, so I faced him. He pulled another towel from the well-stocked pile and dried my hair.

"I bet it's been a while since anyone dried your hair," he said.

"My mother is the only other person who has ever dried my hair," I said, on the brink of tears, or orgasm.

"I love you, Mateo," my voice heavy with desire.

I wanted him to tell me that he loved me, but he was silent, focused on drying my hair. When he stopped drying my hair, he let the towel drop to the floor. He playfully ran his finger through my hair, and I saw him smile. It was a sweet, tender smile.

"I'm glad you think you love me," he said, rubbing his nose in my freshly washed hair, "I remember your beautiful long hair, a tumble of colors, silver, sable, gold and flint all together. It looked like a halo whenever you turned your head."

He never said he loved me, but it was okay that he hadn't. There was a gentle harmony between us, like a pair of musicians long used to playing together.

I'm sure he expected to see me featured on the 5 o'clock news, the victim of a 'street execution' at the hands of the police or FBI.

He reached for my chin, took it, and directed my face up, my mouth joining his, our tongues dancing deeper and deeper. My instincts earthy and natural, wanting this man, wanting him more than I had ever wanted anything in my life.

A rush of hormones, a mammoth wave of sexual desire pushed me forward, knocking aside everything in its path. I couldn't fight the tsunami of desire that overwhelmed me. Instead, I swam with the wave towards him. A harbor of dark hair and burnt sienna skin, I found my body crashing toward him uncontrollably pursuing a mystery not yet revealed.

His eyes molten hot as he ran his tongue along his lower lip. Reaching out, he pulled my skimpy covering free of its makeshift fastening, causing the damp sarong to fall heavily to the bathroom floor.

He picked me up in his arms and carried me into the sleeping area, bare skin against bare skin, and laid me on the king bed.

"I want you to be sure."

His words raised goosebumps on my arms, and I reached out for him. Our lips reignite the fire, and he stoked the embers with long and passionate kisses coaxing and coercing my increasing passion. My hands roamed freely offering tender caresses. He wrapped his arms around me, his heat warming my body. I moaned, closing my eyes, his hand moved slowly up and down my naked body from neck to knees.

He moved, and now I'm the one on top. I hadn't planned on this. His arms are outstretched, and he is with both hands stimulating my breasts and running his hands down my stomach.

"I love watching you," he said, his eyes blazing with sexual passion.

I stared down at him, my breathing coming in stops and starts. He smiled. With another quick motion, I am under him.

"You are so wet I want to go exploring," his voice a husky growl.

With amazing ease, he slid off the end of the bed, while constantly fondling and stroking me. On his knees, he took the edge of the sheet and wiped the sex juice from my pussy lips.

Smoothly and naturally, he pulled my hips close to the edge of the bed, gently bending my knees up at right angles, giving himself total access to my most personal parts. I looked down, across the length of my body and we made eye contact.

"I want you to relax," he said quietly, while gently massaging and kneading my inner thighs. "Just take slow deep natural breaths and let your body become part of each caress, kiss, and movement. Cunnilingus must be savored and appreciated like fine wine."

He wrapped each of his arms under and around each of my legs and with his hands on my upper thighs spread my legs apart. I felt his breath warm against my skin as he blessed my hungry flesh with tiny kisses. He moved slowly up and down my legs, each kiss a promise of what was to come. His mouth centimeters from my vulva.

I closed my eyes, and breathed deeply, trying to relax, absorbed by this moment of intoxicating excitement. There was no rush, no hurry.

I felt his fingers gently play with my pubic hair. Each kiss a small treasure.

He applied pressure with his hand gently tugging the skin above my pubic bone slightly upward. He teased and taunted me with soft kisses, his fingers raising the tiny hairs on my thighs. I thought I was about to die from pleasure or go insane. How about both?

"You are making me so hungry," he says with a muffled laugh.

His tongue slow and tender took its first lick, going from bottom to top, delivering a mind rocking shutter that shook my entire body. Each lick long and slow, pausing only briefly on the head of my clit.

He guided his tongue as light as a feather across the organ sending shivers along every nerve pathway. His tongue gently, expertly, precisely stimulated my clitoris. My body trembled, my legs quaked involuntarily as his tongue moved up and down the organ loving its hood, its shaft, its base. His precious grazing tongue as gentle and as tender as the wings of a butterfly.

I felt as if I were the center of his being. I was the center of his patient love. His consistent rhythmic pressure delivered throbbing spasms of orgasm.

He embraced me, holding me tenderly. Our mouths united in a long tender kiss.

He moved onto the bed and we lay side by side. He used his index finger to trace mysterious lines across my arm, my neck, my chest. He kissed me gently and then stood up next to the bed.

"Where are you going," I heard myself whine childishly, "Please, I want to satisfy you," I said, baffled and confused, "Have I done something wrong?"

He smiled broadly, "Of, course not. I'm a happy man. Right now, however, I am incredibly hungry. How about you?"

Mateo pushed a small bit of curtain back so he could look outside the room. I could see it was dark outside.

He turned and asked, "How do you feel about Chinese?"

Bewildered and unsure, I didn't answer. I looked at him for an answer as to why he had left the bed. I didn't think this was how sexual encounters played out. Although physically satiated, I thought I had not done my part. And more over, I was still a virgin. What was playing out didn't match anything I had ever read in the magazines.

"You want to do sit down or take out?"

"Sit down."

"Sit down it is."

We found a Chinese restaurant a few blocks from the motel. At the entrance, there was a pool with Koi fish swimming amongst rocks and reeds.

To get to the maître d' desk, it was necessary to walk over a small bridge. The fish swam lazily below us.

I could see pennies laying on the bottom of the pond. I felt in my pocket for a penny, finding one, I tossed it, making a quick request.

Soon it was back to easy conversation and teasing hands on my thigh. I finally understood the meaning of déjà vu.

He was funny and lighthearted, never mentioning my situation, or what would happen to me, or us.

He asked me about my life in Lake Oswego. Was I a good student? What clubs did I belong to?

He made it easy for me to talk. I told him about playing basketball and my interest in genetics. I found myself bragging about being star forward for a team that had won state championships three straight seasons. I proudly told him I was MVP two of those seasons. I left out the bit about being known as "The Spider," and the only female player in Oregon able to dunk the ball with some regularity and even a rare alley oop.

He laughed and asked, "Why only two seasons?"

"My first season they gave the honor to a graduating senior. She was fabulous. Dana Mercer, she's at Duke and will probably go pro."

Mateo laughed and said he was too short at 6'2" to have ever been a star basketball player. Instead, he said he had settled on being a baseball sensation.

I laughed easily at his joke.

"How were your grades?" he asked, "with all that study time basketball must have consumed?"

"4 point, I smiled. Scholarship offers from Yale and Pepperdine," I said with unvarnished pride, "I settled on Yale. It's my Mom's alma mater."

"What's your Mom do?"

"She's a Mom and makes fabulous custom jewelry.

"That seems like a waste of a fine Ivy League education."

"Well, my Dad takes up a lot of oxygen," I said with a giggle. "I mean that in a good way. His career has required a lot of family involvement, especially on the part of my Mother."

"This is the first time we've talked about your family. What does your Dad do when he isn't consuming all the available oxygen?"

I looked away. To be honest, I felt uncomfortable talking about my Dad. It's hard being the child of a major celebrity.

"Don't get me wrong, he is the most kind, generous and thoughtful person in the world," I said, looking across the room to a cluster of other diners.

Mateo was quiet, allowing me time to continue. When I didn't, he asked, "What's wrong? You said he was 'kind and generous,' so I know he's not a serial killer," Mateo said when I didn't continue.

"My Dad is Cal Evenson."

There was at least a thirty second pause. His face blank of expression, as if waiting for the message to unite with his thinking mind.

"The Spark?" he asked, surprised and incredulous, "The basketball legend?"

"Yeah, that guy," I said avoiding eye contact. "Can we talk about you?" I said before adding, "I know this whole disaster that has become my life is killing my parents. They had such great hopes for me."

"Okay, what do you want to know? I've told you a lot already," he said, "You know I went to college in New York and graduated from Fordham two and a half years ago," he said. "I want to get into politics. I'm still a bit of an idealist and think I can make a difference."

Interjecting I said, "Living next door to a high-profile politician is living hell," I told him.

I was referencing my last twelve years living next door to Jerry Johnson, U.S. Speaker of the House of

Representatives. Mateo laughed, admitting that he had never thought of it from a neighbor's perspective.

"Your warnings noted. I'd been thinking about making a run for governor of Jalisco State next year, but maybe I should focus on a campaign for the Guadalajara School Board," a grin tugging at the corners of his mouth.

"Quite honestly, you should be a model," I observed, "You could make a fortune."

"Hey, when I was in New York I did that gig. For four years, I studied, and when I wasn't studying, I was posing for all the top magazines. I was on more than two dozen covers. Calvin Klein loved me, and I traveled the world for Versace. I walked the runway at fashion week in Paris, London, New York, and Rome. Women came and went," he sighed giving me a world-weary look before wiping the corner of his mouth unnecessarily with a napkin.

He plunked four quarters in the table-side juke box and spent several minutes making his solitary selections. It was a second or two before I heard 'Black Beatles' start its play. I silently waited for him to continue.

"Just so you understand, I'm an only child. I received a lot of attention. I had a very solid home life. I grew up with strong core values. My parents were nurturing and loving."

Mateo took a bite of his Kung Pow, before continuing, "That solid footing allowed me to see the fashion business for what it is. It is phony to the core. It is especially hard on women. It's an industry where surface beauty is overvalued, and goodness and kindness undervalued. A scar or a wrinkle can be considered attractive on a man, but with a woman it can be career ending. I saw a lot of broken hearts."

He looked at me for a short moment, reached across the table and snagged a bite of my Mongolian Beef, chewing it thoroughly before continuing.

"Don't get me wrong. It was an incredible experience. I made some great friends, some that I still see. But at the same time, I'm glad I was given the opportunity to step in and out of that alternative universe. I was young. It was fun because I saw it for what it was. Some people get all hung up in 'the life,' and it turns out badly for them. Thank the stars, that never happened to me."

I dunked my crab puff in sweet sauce, as 'Tennessee Whiskey,' began to play. I stared at him.

"Lots of money, lots of drugs, lots of sex. How could anything possibly go wrong?"

He laughed, as those memories tugged him back in time. Those thoughts silenced our conversation. I could tell he was remembering a woman.

I said nothing and ate two crab puffs, before "Life Is Good," broke the silence.

"Between an extremely sweet baseball scholarship, and my modeling career, I could afford a charmed life. First-class education, a great apartment in the city, a hot car, and a fat investment portfolio. I never had to ask my parents for any financial help. I'm pretty proud of that."

Despite gorging on the Family Gourmet Combo, we left the restaurant with four take out boxes. Mateo opened my car door for me, and I climbed in. He stashed the take home boxes in an ice chest in the cargo space, before climbing behind the wheel.

"Do you want to do anything? A movie? A game of miniature golf? A walk?"

I looked out the window and then down at my hands. I made a show of looking like I was thinking it over. I didn't want to sound like a slut.

"I want to go back to the motel and fuck your brains out."

His smile took up his whole face and he kissed me enthusiastically and said, "Let's take a walk first."

I heard myself growl involuntarily.

Mateo laughed, and grabbed both of my hands, "I want this to be a special night for both of us."

Chapter Eight

White Picket Fences

Mateo found a station playing smoky blues and let it play.

I reached to him, running my hands up and down his bare arms, waiting for the hair to raise in response to my touch. We leaned together our lips hungry for each other. Our mouths united in a long kiss with tongues touching, teasing playing with one another, feeding our mutual desire. I felt an earthquake shake the ground under my feet.

I heard him whisper my name, as he cupped my breasts in his hands and gently sucked on each nipple.

With easy confidence he moved his kisses down my belly. I felt my skin flush and my whole body stiffen. His hands roamed my skin, arousing every nerve ending. His hands flirted with my thighs, teasing my pubic hair. His fingers trace the edges of my pubic mound, wet with yearning.

He slid off the bed, bringing my ass to the bed's edge. He maneuvered his head over my pussy and buried his face. Long slow sensual licks, stopping intermittently to rest his tongue on my clitoris. I felt his finger stroking the outside of my vagina stimulating and exciting me.

I felt my abdominal muscles tighten. I reached out and took his shoulders, holding on for dear life. My pelvis pushing against his face.

"Don't stop, don't ever stop," I begged, my voice deep and guttural.

With each slow lick of his teasing tongue, I am met with deeper passion, unimaginable pleasure, sweet, exquisite euphoria. I watch as I split into thin slivers. I wonder if I will ever be able to gather all the pieces and put them back together. I tried to speak, but my brain couldn't assemble language.

He moved onto the bed and laid next to me. I turned toward him, and we kissed deeply, and I could taste my sex on his lips and tongue.

I felt the hardness of his dick pressing against my thigh. I took his swollen organ in my hand and began stroking him. I took him in my mouth, I continue the rhythmic motion, as my head moves up and down the shaft. My tongue swirled on the head of his cock with each pass.

In a smooth motion he mounted me. Carefully he directed his rod toward my sugar walls. I raised my hips to meet him, giving a small cry, as he entered me. My body responded eagerly and wantonly. Every molecule, every cell of my body savoring the fullness of him inside me.

He pushed slowly, pressing firmly, ensuring continuous pleasurable pressure against my clit as he broke my cherry. His thrusts were slow and measured, the head of his shaft teasing and introducing itself to every quadrant of my inner being. I moved my hips in a circular motion to enhance the sensation.

"I need to slow it down," he whispered, easing himself to the rim of my pussy.

He kissed my mouth and then swept his breath across my ear lobe and down my neck.

He directed his throbbing head in a spiral motion at the entrance to my love channel. I felt every cell in my body heat up. I winced from slight pain. At first, he was slow and deliberate. Each deeper insertion a promise of more to come.

Soon he is pushing harder, faster, shoving himself into me, thrusting over and over taking me again to that sweet, exquisite euphoria. The edge of another climax.

Thrusting over, and over, he groaned, his legs braced and with a final thrust he pushed deep inside me, reaching his climax with a barely audible, "fuck."

With his last thrust, I moan. My body is tight and seeking relief and exploded in orgasmic release.

94

After a moment or two, he rolled off me and took several deep breaths then plants a big happy kiss on my mouth before he wrapped his arm around my shoulder.

"Holy fuck," his only words.

I silently wondered if his brain like mine had been cleared of all its accumulated knowledge, life existing solely for the pleasure of itself and its mate. He hummed along with "Heart Shaped Box" on the radio, while I nuzzled his chest and belly.

He hugged me again and laughed for what seemed no reason at all. After a couple of minutes, he got up and went to the bathroom where I heard him use the toilet followed by water splashing into the sink.

He came back and sat on the edge of the bed, handing me a warm washcloth and a small towel. I wiped my face and then my swollen sex.

Finally, he asks quietly, "Are you okay?"

"W-hat?" I stammered, trying desperately to reassemble my thinking mind, "I've never been happier. Check out these cheeks."

He gestured to a blood smear visible on the bed linens and the towel.

It was my turn to laugh. I've had nose bleeds that were worse than that.

"I'll wash them up."

"I was referring to you, not the sheets," he said flatly.

"I'm good. Remember the cheeks," I said giving him my best and stupidest grin.

The following morning while Mateo took his shower, I tried to hand press his uniform without success. After laying under a pile of wet towels and combat boots overnight there was little my flattened hand press could do to rectify the situation.

"I hope you don't mind dropping me at the airport by 9:00," he said from close behind me, his arms engulfing me, his hands finding my naked breasts.

I pulled into a temporary parking spot reserved for loading and unloading in front of the airport entry doors. His uniform was badly wrinkled, and his spirit sober.

We had barely spoke since leaving the motel. I cut the engine and he leaned toward me, kissing me tenderly on the mouth.

"I hope by bringing you back to the United States I haven't signed your death warrant," his eyes heavy with sadness, "I think you should have stayed with me in Mexico."

"I couldn't do that to you, someone would have noticed me there," I said with total conviction.

He pulled an envelope from his pocket and extended it in my direction.

"There's $5,000 US dollars. I think you are going to need it."

"No. No. You don't need to give me money."

"Don't argue with me, chica," he said terminating any further resistance, "Take the money, you are going to need every cent of it, and probably a lot more."

"Thank you, I can't thank you enough."

"That's more like it," he said kissing me.

"Mateo, I need to tell you something."

"What?"

"I left something at your house."

His expression went from a smile to a scowl.

"What did you leave?"

"A flash drive."

"Go on," he said, his voice as cold and practiced as any cop.

97

"Several weeks before the Lake Oswego murders Cory downloaded compromising files from Speaker Johnson's computer. Cory gave me and Ward each a copy of those files and kept one for himself."

"The news story is that you and your friends downloaded TOP SECRET files from Jerry Johnson's computer, all in a plot to pull a Wikileaks, except with the Chinese instead of the Russians."

"You couldn't possibly believe that story. I'm no traitor. I'm certainly no hacker. And I sure as hell didn't kill anybody!"

"If I didn't believe that you were innocent your ass would already be in jail."

I looked into his eyes but said nothing.

"So, let's get back to what you left at my house."

"There is a small attic space you can access from the closet of that bedroom I used. There is a dropdown ladder."

"Yeah, I know. You went up there?"

"Yes. I made a copy of the flash drive Cory had given me and I hid it in your attic. It is one of only two remaining copies. It's behind the insulation. Just count over eight studs and you will find it.

"Fuck," Mateo spat.

98

"When you watch it, you will understand why Johnson will do anything to silence me and get hold of what he believes to be the last of those thumb drives. He didn't get to be Speaker of the House by keeping his hands clean.

"Fuck," Mateo repeated.

"I'm convinced Johnson is trying to have me killed, just as I am convinced, he was behind the murders of Cory and Ward. I'm afraid to contact the FBI. He has them all in his pocket."

"You had two fucking weeks to tell me all this. Why didn't you tell me about this when we were in Guadalajara?"

"I don't know. I just wanted to be with you. I just wanted to be happy for a little while. To pretend everything was normal. That you and I were normal. That we would be together. I was daydreaming names for our children. I wanted you, and a life with you. I'm so sorry."

"I don't have any more time. I can't miss my plane."

Still holding me, he looked at me, with an expression I could not define.

"I want you to know this really disturbs me. I'm sure I would have come up with a better plan if I had had this information back in Guadalajara."

"I love you," was all I could say.

He rocked me in his arms for another half minute before he picked up his bag and without a word walked into the airport.

I knew he had risked everything to get me out of Mexico, and I had repaid him by putting his career and possibly even his life in jeopardy.

Chapter Nine

Middletown, Illinois

I had come a long way since leaving Mateo in Laredo, Texas. Twelve hundred and twenty-five miles to be exact.

I'd seen a furnished farmhouse outside of Middletown, Illinois, advertised on Craigslist.

The landlord was showing noticeable distress when I arrived ten minutes late for our appointment.

"Are you Mr. Ryndell?"

"Yes, Craig Ryndell."

He was casually dressed in a tan corduroy sport coat, plaid shirt, khaki's pants, and desert boots. He was lean and handsome with silver hair. I guessed he had seen at least sixty summers.

I'd heard of bad things happening on Craigslist and was cautious. Seven years of kickboxing, plus rough court basketball, made me confident I could handle myself in case Mr. Ryndell had bad intentions. Unless of course he had a gun. If Mr. Ryndell had a gun, it was probably already too late to shift the direction of our encounter.

"I was afraid you weren't going to show up," he said somewhat irritably, "I've come out here from the hotel in Urbana three times this week and you are the first person that has kept their appointment. So, thank you. I need to warn you, my Dad was a pack rat."

"I won't dispute that," I said with a quick scan of the living room.

There were books stacked in precariously high towers on every available surface. Numerous fine animal heads decorated the walls. Apparently, the elder Mr. Ryndell had been a voraciously reading taxidermist.

"Did your Dad die recently?"

"Last month. I live in Santa Barbara, California. The Meals on Wheels driver found him in a bad way and called an ambulance. He was dead before they reached the hospital. He was 96."

"He must have taken good care of himself to have lived to such an advanced age," I said with a tentative smile.

"Damn right. He ran five miles a day until about ten years ago, when a severely damaged tendon put an end to his running days.

"Wow."

102

"So, the old boy, replaced his daily run with two hours of daily lap swimming. In fact, he was seen at the community pool the day before his death, looking strong and healthy."

I assumed any rental arrangement would be short term, thinking Mr. Ryndell, being from California, would want to sell the house.

"To tell you the truth Ms. Cameron, I'm feeling overwhelmed," his mouth slack, his forehead a puckered field of indecision.

"Could I help you do something with the place?" I said, not knowing what else to say.

Volunteerism is an admirable quality and I have found most people respond favorably to offers of help.

"I had a real estate agent come out and look at the house, but she wasn't very hopeful. She told me a little cottage like this, in this condition, would be hard to sell. She called it 'a monument to the hoarder lifestyle'. I told her thank you, but I needed an agent that could embrace the clutter. She shrugged her shoulders, got in her car and drove off."

He looked around, obviously dazed by the fact his father had lived with such disarray.

"What made you think it would be a desirable rental?" I asked with a challenging look.

103

"I'm desperate, Ms. Cameron."

"Why is that?"

"You see, I'm a college professor. Classes are going to start. I have ten days. I'm sorry I've wasted your time. Please, forgive me."

"If I understood what your end goal was, maybe I could help," I said sincerely.

"I want to sell it. Put whatever I get from the sale into an investment and move on. My Dad and I weren't close. We talked on birthdays and holidays. I have my life in California, and he had his life here," Ryndell said with a deep sigh, "I wish it had been different, but it was what it was."

"What if I agree to clean up the property for you, keep whatever I want, and take the rest to the local Salvation Army, in exchange for living here free for six months? We could make this a win-win for us both."

"Well, I'm not sure what all is here," he said clearly weighing his potential profit against the inconvenience of staying in Illinois and going through every box and cupboard.

"No worries. I just thought I could help you out," I said with a casual shrug, minimizing my investment in the potential good fortune.

We stood there locked to our spots.

"You know Ms. Cameron, there is nothing here that I want, or need. You've got a deal if you are sure you want to take this project on," he said his face clear of all doubt.

We took about an hour and worked out the details of our agreement. We put it all in writing and we both signed and dated the documents.

Basically, I could keep, sell, or give away any personal effects on the property in exchange for cleaning up the place. I had six months to get it ready for sale. I could live in the home until it sold, or for a maximum of one year. At the end of a year's time, if the house remained unsold, and I wanted to stay on, we would re-negotiate.

"Well, young lady, I'm thankful you saw my ad," he said with what seemed true relief.

I saw him smile for the first time. It was a nice smile. I was truly glad I could help him and myself. I was unsure whether Zeus, or Craigslist should get the thanks.

He pulled two sets of keys out of his trousers' pocket and handed them to me. From a countertop in the kitchen, he handed me a list of phone numbers for the electric, garbage, and propane service providers.

From his billfold he pulled out a business card with his address and both his work and cell numbers. I watched as he walked around the living room, scanning the clutter before he picked up what appeared to be a handblown glass paperweight and slid it into his pocket. He gave the room a final once over, shook my hand and walked out the door.

I liked Middletown because of its tiny size. It has a wonderful central park, surrounded by historic homes. The little town is just a couple hours from Chicago. To my amazement I had been able to stay under police radar now for over six months.

I saw a recent FBI Files TV show about a Boston crime boss named Whitey Bulger who lived quite well while on the lamb. He was on the FBI's 10 Most Wanted List for over a decade and was on the run for over sixteen years. I wondered if maybe this was going to be easier than I had originally thought. Then again Bulger still got caught and was subsequently beaten to death in prison. Not a sought after ending.

It's hard to think about the future when you really don't have one. Whether Whitey Bulger, Jesse James, Al Capone, or Sky Evenson there comes a time when the future is nothing more than a false dream, or at least an alternate reality.

When my Mom would get anxious, or have an argument with my Dad, she would usually head to her workshop. My Mother has a real gift for jewelry making. She doesn't need a lot of excuses to escape to her favorite pastime. She is quite resourceful. She creates cool custom jewelry, bracelets, necklaces, earrings, and small jeweled crosses, which she sells for some incredible prices. She is quite famous, in her own right.

She uses recycled costume jewelry, old leather belts and even horse tack in her designs. I have been helping her with her projects since I could stand on a chair and reach the worktable.

Every day I dutifully went through at least a dozen boxes of Johnny Ryndell's property. One of the first things I decided to do, was take the stuffed animal heads down from the walls, as impressive as they were.

In addition to deer, moose, and elk heads, there were numerous stuffed birds. Mostly waterfowl. They were beautifully done and in exquisite condition, despite a small amount of dust.

After cleaning off the dust I called a local taxidermist and asked him what I should do with them. The last thing I wanted to do was take them to the dump.

"Hi. I'm Lori. I called you about the taxidermy specimens I have."

"Hi. Lyle, Lyle Newberry. Whatcha' got?" he asked with an affable smile.

"Well, Mr. Newberry, I brought every item I have. I think they are extraordinary," returning his smile, "They're in my SUV."

"Lead the way."

I opened the cargo gate and he looked in. He picked up each specimen and examined it closely.

"Johnny Ryndell. I know his work well. He was a true craftsman. A real artist.

He picked up the North American Wood Duck specimen, and was turning it around and around, looking at every aspect, mumbling, mostly to himself, "Beautiful. Just, beautiful."

"I heard Johnny had died. It's sad, but he had a good long productive life. Do you have proof that you are authorized to dispose of his estate?" he asked with a casual up and down assessment of me.

"I am employed by the younger Mr. Ryndell to clean up the property and dispose of all his father's personal effects. I have documentation to show I have the right to sell the items, if that's what you are asking?"

"That's what I'm asking," he responded flatly.

I pulled out my paperwork and after a short inspection he seemed satisfied.

"If the price is right, I'll take it all. How much?"

"Make me an offer," I said with growing confidence.

He was still lovingly holding the Wood Duck in his hand, apparently bonded to it.

"Well, that elk head is a phenomenal piece, and this little baby is exquisite."

"How about $4,500?" he asked, looking down at the Wood Duck.

"How about $6,000?"

I knew that Lyle was sure he had a treasure trove.

"I can't do six. I'll do $5,200."

"Sounds great," I replied smoothly, hoping to maintain my calm demeanor while I was jumping up and down inside with glee.

"Be cool, look cool," I said under my breath.

"You've got a deal, young lady. I'll need to copy your paperwork and I'll write you a check."

"A check? I can't take a check. I am just here for a short time and don't have a local bank account."

"Okay. You'll have to go to the bank with me. You alright with that?"

"Sure, no problem."

Chapter Ten

Salvaged Treasures

Shortly after moving into the Middletown cottage I did a bit of exploring. When I was in the Goodwill Store in Urbana, I saw several bags of costume jewelry for five bucks a sack. I grabbed up all three bags, threw them in the cart and headed to the men's clothing section and grabbed every leather belt they had.

There was a small outbuilding on the Ryndell property that I decided I would turn into my jewelry workshop. I spent a couple of days cleaning it out and hauling unwanted things to the dump, the thrift store, and the Senior Center.

Under all the junk I uncovered a fabulous work bench, and a dozen separate small bins. I divided my supplies into the bins; one for metal, one for leather pieces, one for wire and rivets, and so on.

In a single afternoon, I went from thinking about getting a job, to starting my own jewelry business, which I christened, "Salvaged Treasures."

The tools are simple and inexpensive, the recycled items are basically given away, and the process is easy, and the product sells. The combination of those factors encouraged me to go for it.

Who wouldn't want to be their own boss, unless of course, they have access to a large trust fund? I thought that such a plan was safer than a boatload of job interviews. Even a quickie background check had the potential of uncovering dangerous information.

I created several sample pieces and took a bunch of pictures and put together a catalogue. When that was done, I printed up some order sheets and I was in business.

Next, I took to the Chicago pavement. I'm good at this jewelry making thing and have made some very cool stuff. But selling takes a different talent, and I wasn't sure I could pull it off.

I should have had more confidence. My products were soon featured in a dozen Chicago area boutiques and trendy shops. The money was good. I was thankful for that. I also recognized I was becoming too complacent. Too content.

Staying in Middletown much longer had become unthinkable. I liked the little farmhouse with its rural quiet and the basketball hoop in the driveway. Comfortable however was not smart considering my situation.

The media blitz had cooled down. It had been months since I'd seen my face or heard my name in the media. I had started to feel normal, yet at the same time I had never been more scared.

In just over two months, everything in the little farmhouse had been sold, given away, or kept by me. I brought a beautiful Persian rug that I found rolled up in the garage and laid it on the dining room floor. I painted the wood dining set and its matching sideboard. I rearranged the furniture for a more inviting look. The house was now "adorable" by anyone's definition. I was convinced that any realtor would be happy to list the house and its sweet ten acres.

I kept the $5,200 from the taxidermy sale. There was a tractor under a tarp in the barn that I sold for $6,000. I got $2,800 from a collector for three watercolors and two oil paintings and found $500 in a tea cannister. Bonus time came when I found a small fire safe in the bedroom closet.

The combination was written on a piece of paper and taped to the front. Hallelujah! When the heavy door popped open, I was gifted with $1,500 in twenties and fifties.

I stuck most of my money into Ryndell's safe. I kept $2,000 out of the safe and took a few minutes and sewed it into the lining of my parka, just in case my safe and I were separated when the day came that I had to make a run for it.

The younger Ryndell had said that there was nothing he wanted, but I doubted that. I suspected he was just unable to deal with the situation. So, when something special revealed itself, I put it aside so I could send it to him later.

When I was done, there were two good sized boxes filled with items I thought might have financial or sentimental value for Craig Ryndell, including a ring I found in an overcoat pocket.

I'm extremely familiar with costume jewelry and I knew immediately the ring was the real thing. I put the diamond ring in a small jewel box along with an appraisal I had gotten from a local jeweler. I thought that would make his day.

I sent the two boxes of memorabilia to the younger Mr. Ryndell via UPS. In a text I told him I wasn't sure how much longer I would be staying, but I wanted him to have the house keys, which I had packed in one of the boxes.

Under the old man's bed, I found three guns, a Rohrbaugh R9 Stealth Elite semiautomatic handgun, a .22g Winchester rifle, and an Atchison SA .12g shotgun. There was enough ammunition for a good old-fashioned standoff. Ask and you shall receive was my only thought.

See what I mean, everything was going way too good for someone on the FBI's 10 Most Wanted List.

A thick cloud bank hung over Lake Michigan as snowflakes fell intermittently. I pulled up my hood and removed my gloves from my parka's pocket and put them on.

Despite the weather pedestrian traffic was heavy on the Magnificent Mile.

I walked into the Odyssey Boutique at quarter after twelve. Barry hurried to meet me. Barry Simpson was tall, slender, and robust. He claimed to be quite an athlete. He told me he had climbed Mount Everest and Nupsi, swum the Chun's Reef to Waimea Bay event, and biked the Dirty Kanza 200.

I had no idea if he was bullshitting me, or not, but his stories were amusing, and he kept me entertained whenever I stopped by the shop.

"Lori, my dear. So wonderful to see you," he said sweeping me in his arms. I followed helplessly as he led me in a spontaneous happy dance.

"Great to see you too, Barry."

We stopped and he gave a belly laugh, gesturing me to sit, while he claimed the edge of an adjacent overstuffed chair.

"I have news for you my sweet,"

"What kind of news Barry?" I asked trying to keep my face bright and smiling.

"Well, a couple weeks ago, a gentleman called about your jewelry line. He said, he had seen one of my ads that featured your beautiful pieces."

"I didn't know you advertised."

"I advertise in several national magazines, and on the internet. You don't think I keep this place running by foot traffic, do you? I have quite a successful online presence."

"Honestly, Barry, I never thought about where your business came from," I answered idiotically, my mind racing.

"He didn't buy online, however. He came into the shop. He said he was in town visiting for a couple weeks and wanted to check out your stuff in person. He examined it closely and seemed quite impressed. He bought everything I had. Half a dozen bracelets, a dozen pairs of earrings and four of your necklaces. I gave him one of your business cards, but he said he wanted to meet you, face to face."

"He bought everything you had?" I asked warily.

I wasn't sure if the news was a good thing, or a deeply troubling one. With racing heart, I swallowed past an ostrich egg that was lodged in my throat.

Every unusual circumstance caused my paranoid brain to lurch into overdrive. I watched as Barry walked around in front of me rubbing his palms together.

"Anyway, he called a couple of days later. He told me everything he had bought sold out within hours of putting it on display."

"He told me his mother owns two high-end shops in Manhattan. She is convinced she can sell everything you can send her."

"Manhattan."

Realizing I was less than enthusiastic, he looked at me quizzically.

"You don't seem excited. You should be jumping up and down. What's wrong?

"I can barely keep up with the orders as it is. I can't commit to do anything more. Quality will suffer," I said with true conviction.

"This is a fantastic opportunity. Just hire someone to give you a hand," he said, his joyous mood deteriorating quickly.

"No," I said, "I will not hire someone to help me, and I will not take on any new clients unless I reduce my outlets here."

I heard myself but couldn't believe my own ears. My clients were all moving as much product as I could provide.

"You could more than double your return. Drop two of your Chicago firms and go to Manhattan," he said hugging me affectionately.

"I need to think about this, okay?"

I reached into my messenger bag and pulled out a package.

"I have your order, and the invoice. You owe me $625.00."

"Sure, hon. I want to look at what you brought me,"

Unwrapping the manila wrapped box on the counter, he appraised my handiwork.

"Awesome, just awesome."

He pulled out his wallet and counted out $625.00 and handed it to me. I signed 'paid in full' on the face of the invoice and handed it to him.

"I don't want you to be mad. But, ah, ahh, I took the liberty of telling Hayes you would be coming in today."

"What?!" I heard myself squeal, as I clenched my jaw.

"I want you to seriously think about this opportunity," he said with a conspiratorial smile, "You have the talent to go big. I mean that. Don't fear stardom, you are made for it."

"I feel like you have me on the auction block," I said barely able to conceal my irritation.

"Sometimes the artist is the last to know how great their work is," he gushed.

The last thing I wanted was to draw attention to myself. Talk about unwanted success. I expelled a gasp of air and felt limp, wondering if they would want photos of the artist. Fuck, yes. The more pictures the better, I thought anxiously. I was afraid my little dance with infamy was about to end in a bad way.

"I need to think about this," I repeated, waving my arms uselessly in the air, "I'll call you next week with an answer."

I couldn't help but notice him when he came in. My hot guy radar was fine-tuned and working perfectly. He had a GQ wardrobe and a face made for the movie screen. I watched him for a minute. Then Barry grabbed my arm.

"That's Hayes. Let me introduce you."

"Sweet Odin. How could you have done this?" I whispered.

118

I watched as he moved toward us. When he stood in front of me, he gave me a blatant sexual scan before turning to Barry.

"Barry, is this our artist?"

"Yes, Hayes. Let me introduce you two. Turning to me, he said, "I want you to meet Hayes Benton. Hayes, this is Miss Lori Cameron."

We shook hands. His eyes were turquoise blue and his hair blonde. His tan suggested winters in Barbados, or some other sunny retreat for the rich and famous. His jaw was strong and his lips sensuous. His eyes penetrating. I felt as if I had just stepped off the edge of a mountain, falling in slow motion, past ragged cliffs, destined for a distant impact.

"So, Lori," pausing for a minute, boring his eyes into mine, "Barry tells me you are a college student."

"I'm only taking a couple of night classes at University of Illinois," I mumbled, having forgotten I'd told Barry I was enrolled in classes.

"I assume Barry told you I wanted to meet you."

"He just told me," I said sending a Barry an icy glare.

"Well, to keep it short, my Mother owns two high-end boutiques in Manhattan. I shared some of your jewelry pieces with her and she sold out almost immediately. She

119

thinks you are a genius, and she believes she has a market for all the product you can deliver."

"I'm a designer, I design jewelry and fashion accessories. I don't think I'm a genius," I laughed.

He ignored my retort.

"Are you self-employed? You look pretty young to be an entrepreneur," causing a crease to form between his eyebrows.

"I'm twenty-three. How old are you?" I asked spontaneously, unable to stop myself.

He hesitated, his eyes narrowing, before answering.

"I'll turn thirty next month."

Barry went to help a customer, leaving me alone with the amazing Hayes Benton.

"I'd like to take you to lunch. What do you say? There's a great place just around the corner."

Mateo was the last man I had been sexually attracted to. Until today that is, when I saw Hayes Benton enter the shop. The sight of him awakened my inner Aphrodite, sending estrogen rampaging through my blood stream at hyper-speed. For the first time in months, I felt the chest pounding excitement of sexual desire.

His hands were manicured, and his voice was as smooth as warm honey. His tailored jacket and silk shirt were Gucci. His cologne was Tom Ford's '*Fucking Fabulous*,' and it suited him perfectly.

Chapter Eleven

Eagle's View

When we walked out of Annie's, the snow had stopped, and a wary sun tenuously emerged from its hiding place.

"Well, thanks again for lunch," I said, not quite sure how to disengage from this incredibly attractive man.

"Do you need a lift? I have a car," he offered.

My train leaves at four. I'm going to go window shopping."

"It's too cold to be window shopping," he chided.

"I'm open to suggestions," I said hoping for a wedding ceremony.

"Come on, we can figure it out in the car," he said, directing me toward a black Mercedes limo, double parked twenty feet from Annie's front entrance.

Strange, I hadn't noticed the car before. A formally dressed chauffer hopped from behind the wheel and opened the back door for us.

I'd ridden in limos before with my Daddy, but this was different. I felt my heart skip a beat as I slid into a world of horse farms, dog shows, Lear jets, and decadent island retreats. Hayes slid in next to me, causing an electric shock to arc between us. We both laughed.

"Well, we are both away from home, what should we do?" he asked, giving the question an erotic vibe.

"My friend has provided me use of his place in Winnetka, while he's clearing up some business in Hawaii. The place is beautiful. It's definitely worth seeing. It's historic, but it has all the modern must haves. Full bar, an indoor pool, an outdoor pool, hot tub, wine cellar, ice rink, fitness room, movie theater, bowling alley, ballroom, billiards room, a pontoon airplane, a friggin' toboggan run, all sitting on 125 acres of prime Lake Michigan waterfront."

"Wow. Your friend must be a multimillionaire. Does he let you use his place often?"

"I think gazillionaire is a better description. I've only used the place half a dozen times. I don't do much business in Chicago," he volunteered.

"What do you do?"

His eyes narrowed slightly. There were several seconds of silence before he said a bit mysteriously, "I do global peacekeeping."

My brain raced fast forward attempting to decipher the meaning of his statement, "You're a soldier?" I finally asked in disbelief.

"No. I own a company that protects the richest and most powerful potentates, dictators, autocrats, oligarchs, oil sheiks and any other disgustingly rich fuck who requires top notch security.

I was having trouble correlating security for a "rich fuck" and keeping the peace. In my mind, they didn't easily mesh, and in fact seemed in juxtaposition to each other. As I pondered the incongruity of Hayes' statement, he turned on the sound system filling the passenger area with a soft contemporary ballad.

"How does that equate with 'global peacekeeping?'"

"Well, when one of my clients, who often hold enormously powerful political positions, gets killed or kidnapped, world politics can shift quickly. A big name killing could in fact destabilize a region, an entire nation, or the world, theoretically. My company is big on maintaining stability. No Archduke Ferdinand situations."

Hayes kept the conversation alive, asking me all the typical questions, to which I mostly lied. Not everything was a lie, but most of the small talk was necessarily fabricated, otherwise I would be telling him that I was Sky Bronte Evenson, 18-year-old high school basketball star, fugitive,

124

prime suspect in four murders, recent addition to the Interpol's Most Wanted List with an impressive $300,000 reward on my head.

It took thirty minutes to get up to Winnetka. I watched as we turned off Sheridan Road and were confronted with a black wrought iron gate. The name plate proclaimed, '*Eagle's View.*'

After an appropriately long, tree lined drive, the chauffer halted at the front door of a brick Georgian colonial house, the size of a government building. At the top of the front steps, Hayes opened the door to a massive reception hall with curved central staircase, arched doorways and detailed millwork with views that stretched across manicured gardens to a private beach on Lake Michigan.

A heavy breasted middle-aged woman hurried from a back room. She took our coats and gloves.

"Mr. Benton, I didn't expect you back so soon."

"No worries, Lucy. Ms. Cameron and I decided to come home and find some mischief to get into."

"Yes of course," she said giving me a discreet smile, before hustling off with our jackets.

"Excuse me," Hayes said, and pulled a cell phone from his pocket, as he walked toward a room off the entry hall. I saw him sit down on the corner of a massive desk and talk to the unknown caller. I strained my ears. It seemed he had switched from English to French, but his voice was so muffled I could not be sure.

He had loosened his tie and his demeanor when he returned, taking me by the hand he gave it a gentle squeeze.

"Would you like a drink? I'm pretty, good behind the bar," he cajoled, "Come on, take a chance," he offered me an intense blue-eyed gaze, igniting my sensual furnace.

"Pellegrino, please," I answered.

"How about a Perrier, instead?" he asked, holding up the familiar green bottle for my inspection.

When I nodded approval, he pulled a glass from the shelf, and filled it with ice.

"You robbed me of demonstrating my bartending skills," he smirked, filling my glass.

He lifted a bottle of Monkey Shoulder from a vast assortment of bottles from the world's finest distillers lined up behind the bar. He filled the shot glass and took a slow swallow.

"Why did you come here?"

I had no answer that I wanted to say out loud. There was an awkward silence while I tried to come up with something, I could verbalize.

126

"I think you were deciding if you wanted to fuck me," he said simply, "I saw it in your eyes."

I didn't know if I should admit it, or protest to save face.

"I thought you were hot. I thought about hooking up, but I wanted to find out first if I liked you. I've been in a relationship, and now we are apart. Quite honestly, I am a bit confused and a bit lost."

"Fair enough. That makes sense. Let's see if I can get you to like me," he said softly with a playful wink.

He moved around the end of the bar and sat down on a stool next to me. He raised his glass, and I matched his, "Here's to providence."

"To providence," I mimicked.

His hand caressed my back and I leaned into his touch. I closed my eyes and felt a tension in my diaphragm. I wasn't sure that I should be there, but then I wasn't sure that I should panic, yet, either.

"Do you ice skate?" he asked.

Surprised by the question, I let the question slap against the sides of my cranium waiting for my addled brain to connect with my tongue.

127

"Ice skate?" I repeated with a small giggle, "Not very well," I admit, "I took the mandatory six weeks of lessons. I can sit down and stand up and do backward and forward swizzles, and a snowplow stop. Why?"

"There is an amazing ice rink out here right next to the lake. The views are phenomenal." he said.

"I have no skates," I said.

"Our host has you covered. Every size of skate, times two."

"Are you kidding, me?" I said with disbelief.

"If you prefer, we've got half a dozen Ski-Doo 900 Ace Turbos out in a shed just waiting for someone to throttle them up. We could go boondocking."

"I didn't take you for an outdoorsman. I got the impression you were an urban kind of guy, more comfortable in limo's and Manhattan cafés."

"There you go jumping to conclusions," he said with a sparkle in his incredible eyes.

"Care to expand?" I encouraged.

"Not much to say, I grew up outside of Toronto. There isn't a snow sport I haven't indulged in. Hockey, alpine skiing, cross country skiing, snowmobiling, speedskating, dog sledding, bobsledding, snowboarding, skeleton, ice climbing, snowshoeing, skijoring," he said trailing off.

"Lordy, that sounds like the event schedule at the Winter Olympics. I have to admit I'm utterly amazed."

"Amazed that I get outside," he laughed.

"I just didn't envision you as an athlete."

"At my age, a man needs to stay active. 'Use it or lose it', as you Americans say."

"So, you're Canadian?" I asked, holding his gaze, "Do you speak French?"

"Sometimes to both questions," he said enigmatically.

I said nothing but waited for him to explain. He did not.

"So, sweet cheeks what's your pleasure?" he asked.

"What?"

"Pay attention, I may ask questions," he laughed, a gentle reference to my disconnect from the primary thread of the conversation, "Would you like to ice skate or snowmobile?"

"Snowmobile."

129

"Great."

Hayes leaned over and depressed the call button on a small intercom by the bar.

"Lucy."

"Yes, sir, Mr. Benton."

"Could you find us some outerwear. Miss Cameron and I have decided to go snowmobiling. Hold on a second, Lucy," he turned to me and asked my boot, glove, and snowsuit size and passed them on to the housekeeper.

"I'll go out to the dressing area and find the outerwear. Could you meet me out there in about 10 minutes? I'll have Jeremy bring up the snowmobiles," she confirmed.

I was quickly learning how the other half lived.

Dressed in matching red and black Bogner snow gear, we looked like an ad from the December edition of *Ski* magazine.

Jeremy came in and said the Ski Doo's were warmed and ready and waiting for us out front.

"There's not much snow down here but there's enough to give you traction. Just follow the red flags and you'll be up in the timber and great snow in ten minutes," Jeremy advised.

130

Jeremy was in his late forties with a full head of salt and pepper brown hair and an athletic build.

"Thanks. Would you tell Lucy that we'll be back about 6:00 o'clock, and ready to eat by 7:00 p.m. Tell, her two rib eye steaks, charred on the outside and pink in the middle, two baked potatoes with all the fixings, asparagus tips in horseradish sauce, a mixed greens salad, and strawberry cheesecake for dessert."

"Yes, sir."

I smirked; the whole scenario made me feel as if I was starring in a made for TV movie.

We followed the flags into the timber and found great snow in just minutes. It was thrilling. The views of Lake Michigan were spectacular. There was an abundance of wildlife, challenging terrain, and powder snow, giving us an amazing afternoon adventure.

I hadn't been snowmobiling since the previous winter. Usually, my family goes to Sun Valley over Christmas. My Aunt Janet has a house there and over the holidays it becomes a gathering place for our whole clan. Snowmobiling is part and parcel of those annual excursions.

Hayes was an expert driver and obviously had spent a lot of time in the back country. We stopped at the top of a ridge where there was a spacious viewpoint and we climbed off our machines. We pulled off our helmets and came together to enjoy the view. Hayes put his arm around my shoulder, drew me to him and kissed me gently.

"What do you think?" Hayes asked, as he nuzzled my ear.

"The view, or the company?" I asked straight faced.

"Either? Both?" he said with a laugh.

I turned and gave him a long penetrating scan and then turned my attention back to the panoramic lake view, "Well, I have to admit no matter which way I look the views are spectacular."

Hayes laughed without restraint, pulled me close and gave me a playful kiss on the cheek. We stepped apart quickly and remounted our snow machines.

"We better hustle back or we'll miss a great dinner and Lucy will be madder than a wolf in a trap."

After dinner I needed to unbutton the top button of my slacks just to breathe.

"Are you up to taking a walk?" I asked.

"Sounds like a good plan," he acknowledged.

There was a broad sidewalk that ran from the house to the lake. Tall light poles dotted the edge of the walkway as it meandered around the lake shore, appearing much like any city park.

An invigorating wind was blowing lightly from the north. The sky was clear except for stars. It reminded me of nights in Sun Valley after a day of skiing or snowmobiling. There was a gazebo with string lights and a warming pit that gave us shelter for a few minutes as we snuggled watching the lights from Chicago.

Chapter Twelve

Holding My Breath

"I think it may be time to think about getting me to the train station," I said as we walked back to the house. "I know it is only a bit before nine but the last train leaves just after midnight and I don't dare miss it."

Hayes sensed my apprehension and squeezed my hand as we neared the house.

"Stay the night. There are fourteen bedrooms in this place. We'll find one you like. Jeremy can drive you home tomorrow. All the way home, wherever that is. Forget the train, please."

He coaxed with a little boy grin, followed by a sensual embrace, his hands caressing my ass.

"I guess that would be okay, as long as I get my own bedroom. Right?"

"Absolutely," he said, making a 'cross my heart' motion with his index finger, "I'm a gentleman at all times."

His words made me think of Mateo. I thought I had loved him. I knew I missed him. I had begun to wonder if our relationship wasn't more about the emotions of a young girl and her first sexual experience than real love. There was no reason to assume that I would ever even see Mateo again.

Guadalajara now seemed years away as I faced the reality of a life that had spiraled out of control. There were more and more nights I wondered if I would even make it until dawn. The reality of my situation a daily drag. Somewhere between yesterday and today I had become a cynic and hadn't even noticed.

Hayes was working hard to impress me. I liked that. My brain and my hormones however, seemed to be on separate pages.

"I just don't want any misunderstanding," I said quietly.

"No worries. Let's get out of the cold and we'll go check out the home theater."

He slid his arm around my shoulder, in a reassuring gesture that promised respect and patience as we trudged back to the house.

Back at the house we shed our coats and gloves and went downstairs to the movie theatre.

"Why don't you pick out a movie for us to watch, while I figure out this infernal popcorn machine?"

"I can't eat another bite."

"There are basic laws that govern the universe," he said with a grave and inexplicably serious expression, "one of the oldest and most misunderstood by humankind is that there is always room for buttered popcorn. Especially in a movie theater."

He cracked me up and I found myself laughing stupidly at his comment, probably more from his delivery than the line itself.

"There must be at least 500 movies on a playlist. Lots of recent big budget stuff, and some sleazy stuff too," he said with easy affability, "I'm betting you can find something for us to watch."

"What kind of movies do you like?" I asked, watching while he read the instructions on the front of the popcorn machine.

The machine was a black and gold cart, designed to look like an old-time vendor's cart.

"Car chases, spies, war, and general mayhem. Anything like that will be great," he said with a snort.

"No huggie-kissie love story, with well-written characters, engaging plot and memorable dialogue?

"That's right," he said with a wink.

"There goes '*Jojo Rabbit*' and '*Thor: Ragnarok.*' How about '*Dragged Across Concrete*'? It sounds gruesome and ultra-violent."

"Well, I like the title. Who's in it?"

"Ahh, let's see, Mel Gibson and Vince Vaughn."

"Sounds good, if it works for you."

"It does. That title is quite the hook isn't it?"

Once the popcorn was popped and buttered and our sodas dispensed, Hayes darkened the room and we found seats on a centrally placed couch and got comfortable ready to watch what '*Dragged Across Concrete*' means in Hollywood. Personally, I felt as if the writer had stolen the title from my life story.

Hayes had his arm wrapped comfortably around my shoulder and I felt his nose teasing my neck. While I tried to focus on the dark story of brutal men on both sides of the law, Hayes began his seduction. I turned my face up and we joined our mouths in a passionate kiss, his tongue greedily locked with mine sending electric shock waves to every hungry neuron.

He guided me backward on the couch, our mouths locked in harmless pleasure. I felt his hand moving under my shirt, toward my breast. I put my hand over the top of his to stop him. He gave me a wounded look but accepted the rejection.

"I'll behave myself. I'm sorry."

I smiled and laid my head on his shoulder, thankful that he hadn't pushed the matter. I was having a good time and I didn't want it spoiled by an overly aggressive sexual encounter gone bad.

"I'm not a racist," says one of the characters in the movie, sneering for the camera, "Every MLK Day, I order a cup of dark roast."

The movie is grim and shamelessly graphic. There are places in the action I bury my head in Hayes' chest. The action centers around a pair of brutal police detectives armed with big guns, perfected sadism, and faultless cynicism. The violence on both sides of the law, makes me question just who the good guys are, and not for the first time.

After the movie, I ran around picking up the space, throwing cups in wastebaskets and straightening up the area so it would be difficult for anyone to know we had used the room.

"What are you doing, trying to cost Lucy her job?"

"I just hate leaving a mess," I stuttered.

"Well stop it, you're not the hired help," he said with obvious irritation.

I instantly stopped, realizing I had angered him. His comment gave me a window into how he thought. It was the comment of a man who had never known anything but great wealth and with that great wealth came an elitism that I had never seen before close-up.

Granted, my Dad was a pro athlete and insanely rich by most standards of measurement, but his parents were working class drones. They had died a year apart before they were even able to retire. Sadly, they died before my Dad achieved significant wealth or international fame.

My Mom's parents were also working-class folks. They had at least been lucky enough to make retirement.

Wanting to quickly change the direction of the interaction I tried to shift the conversation away from me and my tendency to take on menial tasks.

"I'm curious, is Hayes a family name?"

"Well sort of. It was my Grandmother's maiden name. So, she had my Mom hang it on me. It's a nuisance. People assume it's my last name, and that Benton is my first name. It leads to endless confusion."

"I wonder if there's another man in the world with the first name of Hayes."

"I hope not. I like thinking I'm one of a kind."

"Let's see if we can't find a bedroom for you," he said.

"Just about anything will do as long as there's a bed and a shower."

We progressed along the upper hall, opening doors, and peering into a series of beautiful bedrooms, each with its own private bath. At the end of a long hall, he swung open a set of double doors to the master suite.

The master suite was the size of the average man's house. One wall was all windows to the lake with a gigantic deck. Another wall sported a fireplace with a large sectional couch in front of it. Across from the wall of windows was the bed. It was obviously custom made, being twice the size of a standard king.

The last bedroom we looked at was next door to the master suite and was especially appealing with a superb lake view and beautiful private deck.

"How about this one?" I asked.

"I'm glad that you chose the room next to mine."

I returned his smile, suddenly aware that I wanted to kiss him.

Hayes apparently felt the same sexual urge and pushed me against the wall and gave me a nasty kiss. The intensity of his kisses became increasingly erotic and demanding. I wondered if he would stop if I insisted. I was sure he would, and because of that I joined the intensity of his passion as it became my passion as well.

My body pressed against the firmness of the wall gave a small shudder as his tongue explored deeper and deeper into my mouth. He bit my lip making me squeal. He covered my mouth lightly with his hand.

"Shhhh, baby, shh," he cooed, his eyes fixed on mine, "I've made an executive decision. I'm not going to let you sleep alone tonight."

He teased my breasts through my shirt. I made no attempt to stop him. He took my hand and led me back to the master suite.

My body quaked as his fingers moved slowly unbuttoning each button of my shirt. He casually unhitched by bra in one smooth motion. I gulped for air, certain that I was going to suffocate.

He tugged at my flesh, little, tiny tugs, making me squirm as his tongue circled my rigid nipples. I moaned softly, running my hands up his arms, gripping his biceps.

Hayes ran his warm palm down my belly and unzipped my jeans. I felt my pelvis move toward him. I gave an involuntarily groan. I stood naked except for my black lace panties. He took hold of my hips, pushed me back a step, so he could look at me.

I leisurely unbuttoned his silk shirt, slipping it over his shoulders, tossing it on to a nearby chair. The shirt was followed by his V-necked T-shirt. Without the T, I could see a huge elaborately detailed tattoo of the rising Phoenix across the expanse of his muscular chest.

He pressed against me. He slid his hand inside my panties. He held his hand on my mons without moving, sending quaking waves across my pelvis.

He began playing with my pubic hair, a slow tease. I raised my face to him and kissed him eagerly. His fingers delicately crossed my pubis and glided tenderly across my clit and into my tight wet crevice. He slid a second digit into my sex and moved them slowly in and out. My body actively responding to his increased sexual stimulation.

I felt the edge of the bed with the back of my knees as he directed me to its pile of pillows and goose down comforter. I kissed first his stomach and then his chest, raising his nipples to rigid firmness. I undid the top fastening of his black slacks, and then inched the zipper down. I took his hips in both hands and eased his slacks down, allowing them to drop freely to the carpet.

I could see the firmness of his arousal through his form fitting undershorts. Sensuously, I grasped the waistband of the black Frigo's and pulled them down. He stood naked and confident. His skin golden, every muscle toned and tight, teasing me with his rigid erection.

"Just what is it you have in mind?" he asked, his voice husky.

I reached out. My eyes fixed on his. I could hear him suck in a deep breath as I spit in my hand and took hold of his rock-hard shaft. My mind nearly went black as my hand moved up and down the length of him. I pumped him several times before I directed his dick into my mouth, wrapping my lips around his sweet warmth.

I felt him tense as I teased. My tongue ran laps around the head of his cock as I sucked. His eyes an azure sea, drown me in their depth. His breathing turned ragged as I moved my mouth up and down the shaft, pushing deeper into my mouth, taking it further and further back.

I felt the pressure of his hand on the top of my head as he stopped the up and down movement. A small gasp followed, as he regained control of the momentum.

"I don't want to cum, yet."

He released the pressure on my head and kissed my hair, and then my ear, dropping little kisses down my cheek, down my neck. His manicured hands cradled my breasts, pulling and tugging on my nipples, sending my body into spasms. I heard myself panting in response.

He moved his stimulation down my body, his tongue, and fingers relentless in their march to the apex of my thighs. A small cry came out as a whimper.

"Shhh. We don't want Lucy coming to check on us," Hayes said with a twisted smile.

My breath was coming in stops and starts, his fingers exploring my sex, teasing, and stimulating me to outrageous pleasure. I moaned, feeling the tensing of my muscles on the precipice of orgasm when he stopped.

He raised his face to mine, kissing me gently, brushing his cheek against mine. I could feel my hips heaving, my groin on fire. He dragged his fingers languidly, from my boobs down my belly. Savoring and prolonging every resulting quivering spasm.

He pressed me back, using the palm of his hand to direct my backward fall onto the pile of pillows. His hand rested on the space between my breasts, holding me down.

"I want you to spread your legs and I'm going to watch you pleasure yourself."

He was down on his knees next to the bed, breathing close to my ear. He kissed his way down to my shoulder, his nose tickling my neck, and down my arm until he was kissing the back of my hand.

"Take your hand and pretend it is my hand, touching you in those secret places, those places that bring you to orgasm. I want to watch. Show me."

I was immoveable, my mind refused to make my hand do his bidding. After an agonizing wait, he lowered my right arm, our fingers knitted together.

He guided my hand across my exposed belly, "You are breathtaking," he said quietly.

I groan deeply and together our hands are sliding slowly across my chest. Lingering briefly, lightly teasing every segment of my naked form. He continued the journey past my waist to my pubic bone.

He lifted his hand, separating himself from me, as I brought my fingers into the wet world of my engorged sex. My back arched and I moaned erotically. He was now the observer, my voyeur, and my lover.

He spread my legs apart, putting his face close to my pussy, breathing his warm breath on my slit, sending twisted coils of sexual energy through me, driving my growing arousal. I continued to moan, raising my hips up and down, joining the urgency of a primal mating ritual.

My index and middle finger entered the swollen channel, rubbing, and stroking. He hovered over me, his mouth pushing away my fingers, running his tongue lightly across my clit, raising an unanticipated shriek.

For the second time he placed his hand across my mouth.

"I want you to be still. You need to learn to allow your body to absorb more pleasure than it thinks it can receive."

He then returned to my crotch, licking, and sucking, my pussy. His eyes never left my face. His tongue on a treasure seeker's journey finding reward in places I never knew existed.

I whined pitifully, when he lifted his face from my wet interior, and pushed a small pillow under my ass, forcing my hips up. I couldn't take my eyes away from his. Swinging over my hips, he was above me. I wanted to reach out and wrap him in my arms but was helpless to move.

"Put your right arm above your head," he instructed.

I raised my arm, and he held the wrist, extending it above my head, resting it against the wall behind the bed where he held it securely.

The muscles at the base of my spine were clenching in a most pleasurable fashion. The sweet sensation of his fingers probing the event horizon had me gasping for air. I was like a diver too long underwater. Each new teasing probe heightening my pleasure. His careful manipulation of my nub by his tenderly moving fingers, caused me to buck mindlessly.

"You are so wet, and so tight," he growled, his voice thick with carnal desire.

"Fuck me. Just, please, fuck me," I panted.

He has his head at my waist, and I felt his warm breath as he moved his head until we were face to face, our mouths coming together in an erotic French kiss.

I felt the warm head of his cock probe the lips of my vagina and I raised my ass to the awaiting penetration. He eased himself into me as I moaned. He pushed slowly with short teasing shallow thrusts. The base of his cock delivering constant pressure and gentle friction. He pushed deeper and harder. His thrusts varying from shallow teasing strokes to plunging thrusts. My body relishing and accommodating his every lunge and jab, until I could take no more, every muscle seizing taut, demanding release.

"Cum for me, baby."

I watched as planets moved from their settled orbits of a billion years until they collided, scattering fragmented matter across the known universe. The force of my climax filling the void.

I watched a wicked smile spread manifest as he felt the intimate collision of flesh, firing hot and then exploding leaving me spent.

He continued thrusting, pushing ever deeper into me. Pounding rapidly, each thrust becomes harder than the previous one. He groaned, pushing himself deep into my hidden recesses. With one final jab and a guttural gasp, he was sucked into his own singularity.

Hayes took several seconds to catch his breath before disengaging with me. He propped himself on an elbow, looking at me with teasing eyes.

"I knew I could make you like me. I just needed a little time," followed by a playful kiss to my bare breast.

He held me in a comfortable embrace, nuzzling my neck with tender kisses, our hands locked together. For a few minutes I felt at one with him and the universe. It didn't feel like a one-night stand.

Chapter Thirteen

Reckless

"What time is it?" I asked, lightheaded and a bit disoriented.

He picked up his slacks from the floor, retrieving his cell phone from the back pocket.

"It's one a.m. That makes it close to twelve hours since we met," he said his eyebrows raised in mock horror, causing me to laugh.

"You are a reckless young lady," he said in the middle of a relaxed laugh, "If you keep this up, I may have to spank your little ass," his eyes igniting to smoldering hot.

Tall, broad shouldered and narrow waisted, he said he indulged in every snow sport known to man. I assumed he indulged in every summer sport known to man as well. The more I thought about it, the more convinced I became that I wanted him to spank my ass.

"I know it's late, but would you mind if I take a shower?" I said a bit unsure of accepted protocol in the world of adulthood.

"I don't think I'm going to let you go until I fuck you again," his voice coarse and sexy.

"Then fuck me."

The expression on his face grew sinister. His hand moved straight to my pussy, his fingers gliding into me while I push against his palm.

"You're so wet," he murmurs with satisfaction.

"Please," my voice nearly panting, "I want you inside me."

He turned me over and yanked me up on to all fours. I flinched, terrified, at first, he was going to fuck me in the ass. Instead, he slid inside and gently fucked my love channel from the back. His hand massaged and teased my clit while he fucked me.

I yelped with delight when he slapped my ass hard. I wanted to scream, but knew Lucy was lurking somewhere in the house. I bit my lip and shuddered, holding back my orgasm, waiting for him to catch up.

He gave several quick huffs of breath, and I felt his body begin to tense. With three deep rapid thrusts, together we fall inward toward our shared blackhole, at the speed of light, confirming all the laws of physics.

"Whoever says you aren't a romantic just doesn't know you," I teased, dodging a pillow he tossed.

I stepped in the shower and heard Hayes come in and use the toilet. To my disappointment he didn't join me. I guessed he was worn out, after all he said he was nearly thirty.

After toweling off I stood in front of the mirror. To tell you the truth, I'd gotten used to my thinner figure and now embraced my sleeker lines.

While I debated, which train I should take back to Middletown, I realized that Hayes was talking on his cell phone. It was late, but the time wasn't the same everywhere, I realized. Hayes had said his company had international operations.

Through the crack between the door and the frame of the nearly closed door I could see him sitting on the corner of the disheveled bed. I hadn't heard the beginning of the conversation,

"No worries, Jer. We're cool here."

There was an extended silence while he listened to the voice on the other end of the line, before he spoke again, "Fuck, no. You're not setting the schedule. I've got time. I've got all the time in the world. There's no need to rush this thing. Just because you screwed up man, doesn't mean I'm going to."

Was he talking about me? Who was Hayes Benton? I suddenly worried that I may have just fucked a man who planned on putting a bullet in the back of my head.

151

He was obviously not a cop, or FBI. It was also unlikely he was a bounty hunter. Maybe he was just who he said he was, a private contractor who solved problems for rich, important people when they needed a little help. Who more perfect to clean up the Speaker's mushrooming mess?

It looked like I could stop worrying about how good things were going and start worrying about how bad things could get.

"Hey babe, you okay," Hayes asked from outside the bathroom door.

It was then that I realized I had been in the bathroom far too long, trying to gather my thoughts and rein in my emotions and slow down my racing heart.

"I'm coming in," he said flatly.

He was dressed in stonewashed perfectly fitted grey Salvatore Ferragamo jeans, and a form fitted black T-shirt, and no shoes.

I stared at him over my shoulder in the mirror. I was both mesmerized and terrified.

"I have no clean clothes or toothbrush," I pouted.

"My buddy is a single guy, but he must get surprise guests on a regular basis, because there's a whole wardrobe full of women's clothes, in the master closet."

I laughed, imagining that a gazillionaire didn't have much trouble finding women who would go home with him.

He reached out and ran his hand along my arm.

"You are really thin, but I'm sure we can find something that will work. We've got toothbrushes too. There's at least a dozen brand new ones, still in their packaging in the top drawer."

"Thanks," I said helpless to come up with anything intelligent to say. My mind raced, but there was no useable thought.

"Well, I guess we better check out the closet. I'm feeling a bit awkward walking around in a wet towel," sounding as childish and petulant as I could.

Hayes led me to the walk-in closet. It was the size of a whole department at Bergdorf Goodman. The labels included such spendy designers as Hermes, Oscar, Alexander McQueen, Valentino, and Vuitton. There was also an arsenal of shoes and handbags from Gucci and Jimmy Choo.

"How about a pair of sweats?" I asked, though some of the McQueen pieces were tempting.

"Let's check the drawers."

The drawers had everything I needed. I found clean underwear, a pair of snug fitting Robert Cavalli jeans and an Amiri sweatshirt.

"I'm really glad you decided to stay."

"I think I need a sugar infusion," I blurted out.

"Great idea, lovely lady. Let's go putz around that million-dollar kitchen and see if we can find something besides buttered popcorn," he said good humoredly.

Hayes squeezed me warmly, nearly convincing me I'd misinterpreted his cell phone conversation. Maybe he wasn't planning to put a bullet in the back of my head. His blue eyes were kind, and his demeanor intimate and relaxed. His hands slid down my back, settling on my butt.

I laughed and turned around inside his embrace and gave him a gentle kiss. He deepened the kiss, and I felt my body defying my brain as I pressed sensuously into him.

"Let's go see if we can find some ice cream," he said, reaching out for my hand.

"You certainly dress well," I said, referring to his Ferragamo's.

"It helps me meet women," he said matter-of-factly.

"I'd say it works exceptionally well."

"Not really, I was just kidding, I don't know why I said that?" trying to explain himself.

"Don't be embarrassed," I said, with all seriousness, "it works."

"My sister is an editor with Vogue, London. She's always sending me 'model samples' from photo shoots. I haven't bought clothes for at least ten years. In fact, I'm forbidden to mix, match, or combine the new stuff with any existing items. She sends me everything from a shoot together in one box. She includes pictures so I get the *'feel'* of the outfit."

He looked me in the eye and smiled sheepishly, before continuing, "Truthfully, if I had been left to my own devices, you would not have gone to lunch with me," he confided with earnest embarrassment. "After I wear an outfit once or twice, I disobey her edicts and mix and match whatever I damn well feel like."

I laughed, knowing that someone else dressed him, as though he were a little kid.

"According to her, I'm the perfect model size," he laughed adding a teasing strut to his walk.

"I'm in total agreement."

As we set out on our ice cream safari, it all seemed so normal, so natural. Inside, I am nearly crazy with fear and

155

confusion. I had trouble imagining Hayes as a cold-blooded killer. But then, I had trouble imagining him an athlete, yet he was, a superb one.

My mind turned to Cory and Ward's murders, wondering fearfully if Hayes had played any part in that gruesome event.

On the surface, Hayes was an exceptionally good looking, rich guy, charming, affable, and harmless. But I was beginning to fear there was much more to Hayes Benton than he was revealing.

He was clearly a man used to camouflaging his emotions, his intentions, and his secrets. That's what sociopaths do. If he was acting, he was giving an award-winning performance. I could only hope that my performance matched his.

Stupidly, I had begun to like him a lot.

I desperately tried to slow my fibrillating heart and deepen my respirations, fighting off an impending panic attack. I tried to display an aura of easy humor and friendly disposition. I replayed my mantra, "Be cool. Look cool."

Chapter Fourteen

Claustrophobia

Hayes had been snoring lightly for at least thirty minutes. I was convinced he had reached deep sleep. I was exhausted, but I knew I didn't dare fall asleep. I needed to activate my plan to get out of there. If I did manage my escape where should I go? How would I get back to my car? Was it possible I had misheard or misunderstood his cell phone conversation?

My mental guessing game marched on feverishly. Could I go back to the little house in Middletown? I was confident that Hayes had no idea where I lived. I doubted he'd kill me with Lucy and Jeremy hanging about. But maybe they were just props, and they were part of his killing squad.

Still uncommitted to a specific plan I was in ferocious battle with myself. Was it best to sneak away tonight, or wait? No matter what he had said, I doubted Hayes intended to have Jeremy take me home.

I didn't even know where Lucy had put my parka and gloves. It was too fucking cold to be going anywhere in Illinois without good outerwear.

Could I get over the fence if the gate didn't open automatically on the way out, I fretted. I was extremely good at coming up with questions, but painfully inept at formulating realistic solutions.

I cautiously left the bed, moving with stealth, trying not to arouse Hayes. I stood at the bedside, watching his chest rise and fall rhythmically. I put on the body hugging Cavalli jeans and then put on my dirty clothes over the top of them. I buttoned my flannel shirt, my fingers trembling with fear. I sat down on the bedside chair and pulled on my wool socks, and hiking boots. I grabbed the Amiri sweatshirt from off the back of the chair and pulled it on over my shirt. I looked around and found my messenger bag on the dresser, picked it up and slung it over my shoulder.

I turned the doorknob to exit the bedroom, but it was locked. I twisted the knob several times, first one direction and then the other.

"What's up baby?" Hayes asked from the bed.

My heart stopped. I mean I felt it slam to a screeching halt. What could I say to him?

"I have a cramp in my foot. It's driving me crazy. I was going to try to walk it off. I was trying not to wake you up," my voice stronger than I had imagined possible.

"Well, come over here and I'll rub it for you."

I walked back and sat in the chair next to the bed, took off my boot, lifted my foot. Hayes took hold of my foot and rubbed it gently between two hands.

"Why is the door locked?" I asked, just barely concealing my fear.

"Safety concerns," he said definitively.

"What 'safety concerns'?" I countered.

"Home invasion, kidnapping, torture and murder. Extremely rich people believe in locked doors."

"Am I a prisoner?" I asked quietly.

"You are only a prisoner if you think you are," Hayes answered.

I couldn't see his face in the dark, but there was a coldness to his tone.

"I have claustrophobia," I complained. "I'm going to have a panic attack. Please open the door."

"Take your clothes off and come back to bed. I want to get some sleep."

Not knowing what else to do I removed my clothes and crawled back into bed. I felt his arm cross over my chest effectively pinning me to the bed.

The drapes had been opened, and morning light illuminated the room. I noted the bedroom door was standing ajar. Hayes was nowhere in sight. I wondered if he would let me leave.

He stuck his head in from the hallway, "Lucy is going to serve breakfast up here in the community room. She said it would be about an hour."

He was shirtless and his pajama bottoms rode low on his hips. I couldn't take my eyes off the Phoenix rising tattoo that encompassed his entire chest. Damn. I don't think it is appropriate to call a man fucking gorgeous, but he was.

"Okay," I answered slowly.

My heart thumped uselessly. I was too timid to ask if he was planning to release me or kill me.

I rolled over in bed pretending I was going back to sleep. From behind, Hayes pushed my face against the pillows before taking my hips in his hands and pulled me toward his groin.

"Stay quiet," he whispered in my ear.

He turned me over and our mouths met our tongues quickly entangled in a building passion. I took his hardened penis in my hands and rubbed up and down the swollen shaft. He pushed my hand away and stroked the head of his cock across my vulva. My breathing now coming in short gasps. I felt my face flush with desire. Once again, he directed his manhood into me, fucking me until I groaned with joy. His hand covered my mouth, muffling the sound.

When he was finished, Hayes wrapped me in his monogrammed robe and said, "I think I heard Lucy setting up breakfast."

He hadn't shaved, and the blonde stubble gave him the look of a man who flirted with dangerous circumstances. I wanted to reach out and embrace the danger but instead I left my arms at my sides.

"Come on, let's eat," he said taking my hand.

"I was thinking we could go snow shoeing this morning for a couple hours. Burn some calories and then come back to the house and have Lucy feed us lunch. Sound like fun?"

"How long are you expecting me to stay?" the question finally moving from thought to language

He ran his tongue across his front teeth. His eyes were blank.

"How long are you expecting me to stay," I repeated.

"I'll have Jeremy load the snowshoes into the Ski Doos and we'll start our adventure up there where you said you liked the view in all directions," he said with a chuckle that morphed into a full-blown laugh.

I said nothing but sat down in his lap and laid my head on his shoulder. His refusal to answer my question was both unnerving and arousing.

"What do you say?"

"It doesn't sound like I have a choice," I said flatly, followed with a quick irrepressible giggle, "I love to snowshoe."

"Be cool. Look cool," I reminded myself.

"I was thinking this afternoon we could swim for a while and then spend the evening watching a string of porn films."

"Sounds like you have everything planned out. A day full of fun and exercise and a night of abandoned sex."

"That pretty much sums it up."

"Sounds good to me," I said.

I raised my head and found his mouth, tracing it's outline with my tongue, sucking lightly on the sensual lip tissue before inserting my tongue into his mouth. Teasing and exploring, demanding his attention.

Chapter Fifteen

North Star

"Did you ever think I might have a dog or cat at home starving to death?" I asked, looking up from my dinner plate.

"No," he said, "I assume if there was a pet you would have told me, long before now."

"When will your friend be coming home?"

"I talked to him yesterday. He's finished his business in Hawaii. He's in Athens now. He has no plans to be back here until the fall."

Hayes ran his hand across my thigh, making my pussy tingle.

"We have all the time in the world."

I'd heard him use that phrase before. It sent a chill up my spine, reminding me of his middle of the night phone call. If Hayes was one of the bad guys, what was happening between us made no sense. He didn't seem to be on a mission to recover the last known flash drive of Speaker Johnson's misconduct. He did, however, seem like a man with abandonment issues. His eyes never left me.

163

"I'm going to Toronto tomorrow. Pack for an overnight stay."

"I can't get into Canada. I have no passport."

"We'll be landing and exiting from a private airfield. You won't need your passport."

By this time, I had been with Hayes for nearly three weeks. He saw to it that we played all day and fucked all night. Admittedly there was a gentleness to my captivity. I expected that had something to do with the fact that I did not resist him. The knowledge that I was under his control heightened my sexual anxiety and had admittedly enhanced my sexual experience.

I had made no effort to leave since that first night. Once I realized Jeremy was not taking me home "in the morning" I decided the best chance I had to get away was to convince Hayes I was content.

He had to believe I wouldn't try to escape. I had to convince him that I would not run away. I spent every minute working to persuade him I would not try to make a break for it. It had to be done with actions and not words. Never words.

I knew I could get away I just needed to bide my time and be patient. There would be a point in time that he took his eyes off me. I just needed to be ready for that moment.

"*North Star*" was a massive estate. We landed on its private airfield.

Dinner was served at 7:00.

"I bought you a present," Hayes said.

"Thank you. What's the occasion?" I laughed, taking a brightly wrapped package from his extended hand.

"No special occasion. I just thought you might enjoy this. But don't open it yet."

"Okay," I giggled.

"We have an incredible horse set-up here. I want to take an early morning ride, western saddle."

"Okay. I'm a bit rusty," I warned him.

"Just remember to use those incredible thighs to hold on for dear life," his eyes sparkled.

The house was enormous and can best be described as Medieval. Our room was fitted with an oversize four poster bed that had restraints at each corner.

"I'm going to get us some music, "What would you like to hear?"

Sensing his dark mood, I suggested, "Sabbath, Maiden, Darkthrone."

165

He gave me a quizzical look, "That's some really old stuff," dismissing my suggestions with a snort, "I think I'll take charge of the music."

I watched while he did a playlist search and waited for his music choices to start.

"Are you planning on tying me up?" I asked as nonchalantly as I could.

I walked around the bed, examining the black leather restraints.

"I haven't decided yet. Open your gift."

I opened the package and found an engraved vibrator. It was engraved, 'Love. Hayes'. I comforted myself with a laugh, trying not to think about the chains and the possibility of being under his complete control.

I focused on the word 'love' and looked at him.

"I charged it," he offered.

"Thank you. I've never used a vibrator, or even seen one. I guess I need to get out more," I said feeling childish, stupid, and inexperienced.

His expression was bemused and openly surprised, "In the future, you'll never want to be without one."

166

Hayes had my back pressed against the wall when he ripped the buttons off my blouse and reached his hand inside to my lace bra, his fingers kneading my breast. His knee pressed urgently into my groin.

He pulled my face to his mouth and he kissed me more aggressively than ever before. He tore the fastener to my slacks, and they fell to the floor. In a single motion my bra was off and discarded.

"Take off your panties," he said roughly.

I watched him moisten his fingers in his mouth just before he dropped his hand to my crotch, exploring my pubic region. His fingers moved in and out of my wet girlhood, pressing against and teasing the boatman.

He told me to sit on the bed and I did. His eyes searching mine for my response to each movement. He dropped his pants, and I loved his nakedness. His broad shoulders and chest, his narrow waist, his long athletic legs, his tattoo, his perfect body. I reached for him, first sucking, and licking his balls gently massaging, stimulating, and teasing.

He pulled a bottle of oil from a bedside drawer and poured some on my extended palm. With an index finger I drew small circles around the head of his cock and then licked across it with a gentle teasing tongue.

Without warning he pushed my head down hard on his shaft and began using my hair to move my head up and down the length of his cock. First slowly and then more rapidly, each push deeper. With one final push he held my head down as he came in my mouth. I swallowed fast, not wanting to waste a drop.

He pushed me over and we lay side by side facing each other.

"I'm going to go down on you. When I think you're ready we'll do some vibrator-play. Since you're a vibrator virgin I need to warn you that the orgasm you have with such stimulation is different than any other orgasm you will ever have."

"I'm not sure," I said slowly, avoiding eye contact.

I felt timid and helpless, unclear as to what to expect.

"I want you to relax. If, for any reason you need me to stop just tell me," he said as if he were conducting a class on the physiology of sex.

"I said, I'm not sure."

He did not answer. He was good at ignoring any protestation he didn't want to hear.

"I said, I'm not sure," I repeated more urgently.

His tongue traveled down my stomach to my mons and played with my lips and clitoris. I felt the vibrator cross my belly and its soft vibrating head move to my upper thighs. I looked down my body and found his eyes on me as he moved the vibrator closer and closer to my vulva. Every nerve in my body, awake and alert.

He had my legs bent and slowly and gently brought the vibrating head to the rim of my pussy, touching it lightly before moving across my labia and onto the clitoris. I bucked violently at the first contact and tried to pull away.

He lifted the vibrator and waited.

"Easy baby," he said rubbing and patting my thigh. "Take some slow, deep breaths. I want you to control your breathing. It's all about your breathing. Zen."

"O-kay," I answered, tossing aside fear.

"Sometimes pleasure is painful. At first, at least," he whispered, nibbling my breast gently.

He rubbed my thighs and moved the toy back onto my hairy mound. I blew out several rapid breaths and melted into the pleasure. Breathing slow and deep.

"I can't stop, I'm about to cum," I said, my voice low and throaty, helpless to the coming explosion.

169

Hayes held me as I came down, gently caressing my shoulders and depositing baby kisses across the back of my neck. After a few minutes Hayes stood and went to the head of the bed.

"I need to get something to drink," he said clearing his throat, "Can I bring you something?"

"Water, please," I said stopping short of calling him 'master'.

The bedroom was really a suite with bath, kitchen, and laundry combined on the third level of the house. There was a massive roof top deck with a view of the distant St. Lawrence river.

He was back in a minute with what looked like a tumbler of whiskey and a bottle of Perrier. He sat on the edge of the bed and took a swallow of liquor while I gulped mineral water.

"I'm going to restrain you," he said easily.

"Please don't hurt me," I blurted out.

"You're safe with me."

He caressed my cheek, "There are three colors. Green means you're ready to go. Yellow means you need to slow down. Red means stop immediately. If you can't speak you are to shake your head 'no' and say 'Nnn, Nnn, Nnn."

I began to sob. I wanted to leave but I was becoming irretrievably entangled with Hayes. I worried he would become bored with my sexual inexperience and discard me. Or the day would come soon when he would demand the flash drive and put a bullet in my brain when I handed it over.

I don't know if I worried more that he would leave me, or that I couldn't leave him.

He ignored my tears and had me on the bed on all fours. He took each individual restraint and placed the leather and chain restraint, slowly almost ceremoniously around first my wrists and then my ankles.

He slapped my ass with the palm of his hand, and I trembled. He slapped my ass again and I breathed slow and deep as he manipulated my butt, slapping and pinching me. Then I felt the lightest sting of a flogger's whip.

"You need to stay relaxed. I don't want you to be afraid. I never want you to be afraid. It's just another sexual experience," his voice warm and reassuring.

I was hovering on the rim of insanity, ready to slip across its threshold into that dark world of voices and rages. If fear could kill, then surely it isn't a far leap to assume that too much sex could drive a person to madness.

He wet his fingers with my pussy juice.

"Sweet."

I felt a sharp bite to my butt cheek before I felt his hand arouse my anal area with my own juices plus lubricant from a tube at the bedside.

He took his time adding fingers to the exploration. I looked over my shoulder and saw him oil his cock. His hands, hot and fevered, slid across my ass, slipping easily between my butt cheeks.

I bucked involuntarily as his fingers teased and seduced the rim of my hole. He entered me with his index and middle finger, all the while his mouth licked and sucked down my back and across my hips. His weight held me against the silk sheets as his other hand found my vulva and rubbed his thumb against my nub.

I felt the head of his dick tease me. He circled the opening watching my response. He put one hand on my back for support and used his other hand to direct his cock into me. Slowly, tentatively he inched his organ further into me. As he pushed forward his hand toyed with my nub causing my ass to move rhythmically back and forth.

He grabbed my hips and forced me further onto his shaft. I felt him stiffen as he climaxed.

He stood behind me for several minutes after he ejaculated rubbing my ass, kissing my back, my neck, and rubbing the inside of my thighs.

"I'm going to take a shower. Do you want to join me? Or maybe I should just leave you here."

"If I'm tied here, who's going to wash your back?" I asked playfully.

"Point taken," he said.

I was shaking convulsively as he walked to each corner of the bed and released the restraints. Freeing me, he lifted my chin and kissed me deeply. A kiss as caring as any he had ever given me. Was this the life of slave and slave master, I wondered?

We were up early, and our horses were eager for an outing. We spent the morning enjoying snow covered trails and mist shrouded vistas. Hayes was incredibly intuitive. Aware I was a wary rider he maintained strict control of the horses. We were back safe and sound by noon.

"I'm glad you're a Tomboy," Hayes said with a broad smile, as we dismounted at the barn, turning the animals over to staff.

"Get your gear together, I want to be back in Winnetka before dark."

"Did we come to Canada to go horseback riding just once? I asked with surprise.

"A good enough reason, don't you think?"

173

I nodded but said nothing. I wondered what it must be like to have whatever you wanted, whenever, day, night, or holiday, you wanted it. Hayes clearly had limited contact with the word no.

"There's no chance of staying another night?" I asked sucking on my lower lip and giving him my best Lolita parody.

He took my jaw in his hand and held it between thumb and palm and kissed me.

"Your wish is my command, beautiful lady."

'North Star' has the façade of a mammoth Scottish castle. King James would have felt right at home. The interior was breathtaking with two story high ceilings, interior stone walls, decorated with incredible artwork. Pristine views of mountains and valleys could be seen from every window.

"Well, are you going to tell me something about yourself or are you intending that I continue sleeping with a stranger?" I asked desperately wanting to know who this man was.

"And how about you? Do you intend to be honest with me?" he challenged.

Chapter Sixteen

Night Moves

I stood for a moment in the darkened reception hall, before slipping along the paneled wall and into the first room off the hallway. I opened the closet and found my coat and gloves. I pulled my parka off the hanger and put it on, and then slipped on the gloves. Whatever the manifest result of my actions, I was now committed. There was no turning back; it was now, or probably never.

I checked the hallway for any activity, and when I was convinced it was clear, I pressed my body flat against the mahogany paneling and moved quietly, Ninja style toward the front door.

It was after midnight and I had left Hayes snoring in the master bedroom.

Dashing to the front door, I used the keycard lifted from Hayes to open the door. I was outside and at the bottom of the steps in a series of quick leaps.

I headed to the massive garage. As I approached the building my movement activated a motion sensor light system that lit up the entire driveway. Terrified, I slammed my body against the side wall of the garage, hiding in the shadows of trees and landscaping, giving the lights time to shut off and reset.

I noticed the garage had a standard man door on the side of the building. I tested the door, and it was locked. It opened to the key card.

The interior space was mammoth, with parking for at least ten full size vehicles. A motherload of motor bikes and bicycles dangled from the rafters. There was an array of lawn maintenance equipment at the far end of the building.

I saw a small fishing boat pushed against one wall. I looked in the window of the first vehicle and saw a set of keys on the front seat. I wondered if there were keys in all the rigs and supposed there probably were. Were they gassed up? Most likely, I figured. I assumed that our billionaire host had his own fuel pump somewhere on the property. With a fleet of pricey cars at my disposal, maybe I was going to get a break.

I walked over to the boat, imagining for a minute a water escape. I looked in. On the bench seat I saw a fish bat. I grabbed it and stuck it in the back of my jeans. You never know when you might need a helping hand.

In addition to the black Mercedes limo, there was a white BMW 640i sedan, a gorgeous red Audi convertible, a silver Saab SUV, an unbelievable white and black Bugatti Chiron, a beat up old green Jeep and a beastly looking Hummer H2 Snow Runner. Obviously, our host liked cars.

I assumed they were all equipped with anti-theft devices that could shut me down before I could get outside the front gate. I didn't dare take a chance.

The oldest rig was the 4x4 Wrangler. I thought it was too old, and of such little value that it was unlikely to have any theft deterrents. It looked as if the old Jeep was primarily used for four wheeling around the property. I opened the car door, picked up the car keys from the front seat, and scrambled in.

Just as I was about to fire up the Wrangler, I spotted a classic green Kawasaki Ninja sport bike parked directly in front of the Wrangler.

"Yes!" I said giving a mock thanks to the unseen gods of good fortune.

I was confident there would be no anti-theft device or GPS tracking on the motorbike. My brother and I had ridden bikes since we were kids, and despite the potential icy road conditions I felt the Kawasaki would give me the capacity to go off road if Hayes did wake up and decide to pursue me.

I pulled the sport bike out from its parking space and sat on the seat, getting a feel for the machine. The keys were just hanging in the ignition, like a Christmas ornament. I knew that when I pushed the garage door remote, the sound of the door opening would draw attention to my activity.

I kept thinking, I could still go back in the house, and stop all this nonsense. I was sure he wouldn't do anything

177

until he had the flash drive or grew tired of me. I just knew I had to leave before Hayes Benton morphed into Pol Pot.

"Hey, babe, what are you up to?" I heard him ask.

I hadn't been gone five minutes. Does the man never sleep? The quietness of his entry into the garage left me shocked and ill-prepared for any reasonable response.

I searched for my voice, trying to think of something to say, "Oh, hi, honey. I couldn't sleep," I said inanely, "I just thought I'd come out and explore a bit. I used your key card."

"Well, okay, hon, but it's the middle of the night. We can do this after the sun comes up; can't we? If you want to go motor biking, we can arrange it, anything you want," as calm and cool as any psychopath would be. "Right now, I'd like you to come back into the house with me," his voice careful, calm, and reassuring.

Hayes had clearly read the situation and knew he didn't have much time to pull me back from a dangerous action. With gifted intuitiveness he began to talk me down.

We both knew there were only two ways this situation could go. I would either see the error of my ways, and go back into the house with him, or I would make a panicked run for it.

"Jeremy can build us a fire and Lucy will make us some hot cocoa. How's that sound?"

He was moving tediously slow, almost imperceptibly toward me. It was clear he was making every effort to keep the situation calm and loving. He obviously did not want to spook me.

I dismounted the bike.

"That's it, babe. Come on, let's go back inside. It's cold out here," he laughed shaking his shoulders in a series of exaggerated shivers.

For the first time I realized he was only wearing a pair of slacks, a T-shirt, and slippers. Just as he extended his hand to me, he looked toward the man door, most likely expecting reinforcements in the form of Jeremy.

I took advantage of that mistake and bashed him with all my strength on the side of the head with the fish bat. He folded instantly to the floor. On his hands and knees, he teetered, looking up at me with no expression.

Following my years of martial arts training, I raised my left leg and kicked him solidly in the head just to be sure. He toppled over backwards. He was spread out on the concrete, his head bleeding profusely when I remounted the bike and turned on the ignition.

Despite all that damage, I could see he was fighting to stay conscious. His eyes were glazed. He was covered with blood. I hesitated, not sure if I should leave him, or hit him, again. The wound on the side of his head was bleeding

179

heavily. Blood covered his face, and his white T shirt was now a tie-dyed red and white.

He looked seriously injured. I hesitated, not sure if I should leave him. I hadn't wanted to kill him. If I abandoned him, he could potentially succumb to hypothermia or bleed to death. My mind was at war with itself. The last thing I needed was another murder charge. Jesus, why had I hit him so hard?

"W-w-why, why, the fuck?" Hayes stammered.

He had managed to stand, but he was wavering on the verge of collapse. His body lurched from side to side as he tried to steady himself. He grabbed onto the fender of the Wrangler and leaned on it for support.

I watched as he wiped his right hand across his face attempting to clear the blood from his eyes.

"What the hell, Lori? I thought we were having a good time."

My visions of an American Pol Pot dissolved with his question. At this moment he didn't look like a dangerous sociopath. In fact, for a guy who had just been clubbed in the head with a fish bat and then given a mind shocking kick to the head by his latest sex partner, his demeanor was surprisingly controlled.

Had my six months of fever pitch paranoia hatched into a full-blown psychotic break, I worried. A spasm of fear and confusion shot through me. Had I made a mistake? Had I lost my mind? It was beginning to feel like it.

Hayes had managed to crawl between me and my escape route. I revved the motor, simultaneously activating the garage door opener. As soon as the door raised enough for the bike to clear the opening, I released the clutch, hit the gas, and sped past his wavering figure, out of the garage and down the long asphalt driveway.

In the rearview mirror, I could see Hayes had managed to make it out to the driveway. He had been joined by Jeremy. Jeremy handed him a coat and was now supporting him as he swayed back and forth.

They stood in the driveway, bathed in floodlights watching me put distance between us. They seemed bewildered. There was no evidence that they were motivated to marshal any pursuit effort.

Their delay in pursuing me was worrisome. Perhaps they were going to seek medical attention for Hayes. I worried for a moment that my paranoia had gotten the best of me. Even so, I held on to the belief that I had been right to run like hell. Reassuring myself I had no choice. I had to run. I couldn't just stay at 'Eagle's View' until Hayes decided it was time to get rid of me. No matter how great the sex had been I doubted if we would have a second date.

181

I felt confident that Hayes would not call in a stolen vehicle report, at least not right away. If I were wrong, I could be in big trouble. I did the only thing I knew to do; I headed back to Chicago.

The road was well-travelled, and clear of snow and ice. I hesitated to throttle up the power of the sport bike's engine, instead satisfying myself with a modest 35 miles per hour.

Chapter Seventeen

Me and the Ninja

A pair of headlights appeared in my rearview mirror, coming fast. I couldn't make out the vehicle type, but I suspected it was Hayes. I nervously increased my speed. With increased anxiety, I repeatedly checked the pursuing headlights, spending as much time looking in the rearview mirror as I did to the road ahead of me. I knew now I should have hit him again. I won't make that mistake again.

My heart assumed a dysfunctional flutter. I was replaying his words, in my head. The measured cadence, the soft volume, the tender tone. Maybe I should stop and go back to 'Eagle's View' with him.

I heard the roar of the sport bike's powerful engine humming ready to accelerate on command. I bent over the machine's handlebars as I amped up the pressure on the throttle. The bike picked up speed, moving faster and faster.

The only advantage I'd had at the lake house was catching Hayes off guard. I had been able to manipulate that surprise to my advantage. I instinctively knew I was unlikely to get a second chance.

I thought about Mateo. I was angry with myself, for hopping into the sack with Hayes. What a disaster. How could

I have been so stupid? How could I have been foolish enough to allow him to take me so far from my familiar surroundings, so far from the train?

Hayes could have killed me at any time. I had no idea what twisted game he had been playing. If he was part of the Speaker's extermination team why hadn't he demanded the flash drive and tortured me until I gave it up. That wouldn't have taken long. If that had been his intent. Maybe Hayes wasn't working for Johnson. Maybe I was just a convenient victim for a rich sexual predator.

Despite my increasing speed I knew Hayes was quickly gaining on me. I didn't know the road and had to maintain some caution. Otherwise, I'd find myself in a ditch or creamed against a tree. The Hummer Snow Runner was now dangerously close, pushing me to dangerous maneuvers.

I flattened my body, becoming part of the bike. I twisted the throttle. Fuck, was Jeremy trying to hit me? He was within five feet of my back tire and was about to run me off the road. Catching sight of a dirt road coming up on my right, I prepared to make a fast, sharp turn. At the last possible moment, I swerved off the highway, as the Hummer flew past me.

The dirt road was steep, with about 6 inches of snow cover. I held on tight as the bike skidded recklessly from side to side, sending rocks and dirt flying in all directions. I was able to keep the bike upright and climbed quickly into the safety of deep forest.

I killed the engine and watched the action on the road below. The snow crunched under my boots as I ushered the bike to the side of the road, disappearing into the safety of the darkness.

I heard the squeal of brakes as the Hummer came to a stop past the dirt road turn off. Jeremy put the Snow Runner in reverse and was quickly sitting at the bottom of the dirt road.

Revving the Hummer's engine Jeremy started up the hill. Between the vehicle's headlights and a handheld spotlight directed by Hayes the roadway was as well-lit as the Santa Monica freeway.

Hayes was wearing a knit watch cap covering what looked like a sizeable bandage on the left side of his head.

"Lori. Lori," I heard him holler. "I don't know what's going on, but you can't take the fuckin' bike. Come back to the house. Let Jeremy take you home."

I couldn't tell whether the dirt road was just a short logging access road or was part of a greater system of bike trails that crisscrossed the hillsides surrounding Lake Michigan. I pondered how long I should sit there. As the Hummer lumbered forward up the hill, I knew their spotlights would soon reveal my location.

The pounding of my heart was deafening. There was still a considerable distance between us. The only option I could see, was to reveal my position, and then run like hell. I crossed my fingers and hoped I wouldn't get boxed in.

I took several deep breaths and turned on the bike's engine and the headlight flooded the roadway in front of me. My best hope was that the Ninja, being faster and nimbler could easily stay out front of the Hummer.

"Lori, stop this shit," was followed almost immediately by a series of rifle shots.

I was a moving target in the dark. The bouncing headlights and spotlight created weird twisting shadows amid the forest landscape. I was certain that no matter how good a marksman, there was zero chance of me being hit.

I would just push forward. There was no way the Hummer could keep up with me if I kept the bike upright, didn't panic, or do something stupid. Reassured, I held the best hand, I just needed to play it right.

I heard Hayes holler, "Jer. She's up the hill on the right," another two rifle shots followed.

The snow was a bit deeper as I climbed away from my pursuers, but not so deep that travel was difficult. I hadn't gone a quarter of a mile when I came to a crossroads. I quickly decided on the downhill route. The choice proved to be the

186

correct one. Within ten minutes I was back on the main highway, leaving Hayes and Jeremy far behind.

I did the only thing I knew to do, I opened-up the power of the Kawasaki engine, and raced back to Chicago. I covered the remaining twenty miles in less than 15 minutes.

I felt better back in the city, embracing its anonymity. A stolen vehicle report, up in Winnetka, was unlikely to stir up much excitement in urban Chicago.

I wondered if I should ditch the Kawasaki and hop on the train, but I quickly rejected that idea. I was dressed for the cold and decided to take I-55 out of Chicago. The Kawasaki was a great ride and there was almost no traffic headed south out of the city. My new fear was that my Sportage had been towed from the parking lot at the train depot. That would be no surprise, it had now been parked there for nearly three weeks.

It was an easy two-hour commute to Bloomington. I said a prayer of thanks when I saw the sun break over the horizon as I approached the outskirts of town.

I pulled the Kawasaki into a parking space next to the Sportage. Hallelujah!

I created a spacious area in the cargo area of the SUV by locking the back seats down. The Kawasaki weighed over three hundred pounds, but I was able to maneuver it into the back of the SUV using a 2x6 as a ramp and the help of two passing high school boys, who were both cute and chivalrous.

Despite the risks, I needed to go back to the little house in Middletown. There were too many secrets that I couldn't afford to leave behind. Although terrified, I was sure that Hayes did not know where I lived. To the best of my knowledge the only way to tie me to the Middletown hideout was through the telephone number on my burn phone.

It didn't seem like Barry Simpson had a connection to Hayes other than the one he'd stated. I was comfortable that Barry was an innocent participant in the Hayes Benton introduction. I was glad however that he didn't have any way to contact me other than by my cell phone.

Barry said he had been advertising my line in national magazines and online. Hayes wanted to meet me, because of my jewelry line. How would he know Sky Evenson was a jewelry maker? Could the jewelry be the link?

If he was employed by the Speaker, then he did know I made jewelry, or at least that my Mother was a jewelry designer. I'd been Jerry Johnson's neighbor most of my 'effin life. My Mom's jewelry line was quite successful. She was an incredible artist. Cassie Cornell Evenson was mostly a West Coast phenomenon, but she was a phenomenon, nonetheless.

There was no way to hide her influence on my designs if someone knew what to look for. It seems a far reach, but at the same time it was a real possibility.

I had convinced myself that Hayes knew nothing about the little house. If he had known about the cottage, and he was a killer, it made no sense for him to track me to Chicago. Of course, nothing else he had done made any sense.

Barry told me he had given Hayes my business card which had my phone number on it. With as sophisticated tracking system as his kind of money could buy all he needed was my disposable phone number to pinpoint my location. Maybe, all he wanted to do was make sure the jewelry maker was Sky Evenson. That was possible. But why the last three weeks? Whatever his intentions I didn't want him and Jer to catch up with me here. I gave myself an hour to clear out of the house.

The Middletown house was rural and off the beaten path. Such a location was, seemingly a much better place to get rid of a dead body than a borrowed mansion in Winnetka. I was sure if Hayes had known about the cottage, he would have come here first.

My dead body might go undiscovered for months or maybe forever. I could see Hayes killing someone, but I just couldn't get my head around him mutilating people dead or alive. I imagined a shallow unmarked grave for myself, denying my entire 18 years of existence.

189

I pulled my rig up to the back door, opened the cargo hatch, and left it up. I pushed on the bike and created as much space as I could manage, and then covered it with a tarp. I had decided I was going to keep the sports bike. It would be easy to hide. I decided to keep the bike rather than dump it somewhere. Would this decision lead to a film noir moment? I fuckin' hoped not.

I found a pair of black fitted spandex tights, slid them on and pulled on a clean pair of 501's over them. I found a white T-shirt and topped it with the Amiri sweatshirt. The fragrance of his Tom Ford cologne clung to the garment. I imagined for a moment his fingers, teasing me playfully, unbuttoning and unzipping me toward nakedness. I remembered the tattoo and closed my eyes.

I was nearly ready to move on before I was kidnapped by Hayes. My clothes in two suitcases were sitting near the front door. I stripped the bed and used a duffel bag to pack the bedding. I dumped all the papers and documents from the desk into a box. I put my computer in a computer bag and placed it on top of the box.

I stuffed my makeup and personal hygiene items in a gym bag and placed it on the floor of the passenger compartment. I filled a medium size box with all my finished jewelry products. I knew I could sell the items at some point in time, even if I was on the road. I placed the box in the cargo space.

I ran out to the work shed and dumped every bin of jewelry making essentials into three boxes and then wiped down the entire room. I carried those boxes to the SUV and placed them and the suitcases around the tarp covered motor bike.

I ran back into the house. I charged into the bedroom, got down on my hands and knees and retrieved the three guns and all the ammunition.

Sitting on the cargo deck I took time to thoroughly examine each gun. I had checked them when I had first found them, but now I worried I might need to use them.

Each one was clean and loaded. Old Johnny had been a pack rat, but he had quality stuff and he took good care of it. My family had been going pheasant and chuker hunting in eastern Oregon and western Idaho since before I was born. I had grown up with a rifle in my hand.

I slipped the handgun under the passenger seat and wrapped the rifle and the shotgun in a blanket and placed them barrel down on the passenger side of the front cabin. I wanted them close. Hayes could come driving down the road any minute.

I swept the items from the fridge into a large garbage can and when done I rolled it out to the roadside pick-up site.

I took a damp washcloth, and wiped down all surfaces, hoping to eliminate all my fingerprints. I emptied the waste baskets and threw the refuse into a single bag and threw it in the back of the SUV. I vacuumed and emptied the bag and took it with me. I hoped to eliminate as much fingerprint, hair, and DNA evidence as I possibly could. I didn't want anything to tie me to this location or any other for that matter. I checked my phone for the time and saw I had been there less than thirty minutes. I went through each room looking for anything I may have missed. Seeing nothing but clean and sparkling I was ready to leave.

I jumped behind the wheel of the Sportage and sped down the driveway. I was sorry to leave. I knew I would miss this place.

I sent a text to Craig Ryndell. I told him the house was clean and he could put it up for sale. I advised him I had moved out of the house. I thanked him for the opportunity to live on Dad's wonderful property.

It was pushing 9:00 a.m. when I pulled onto I-74 and began watching for I-90. Within fifteen minutes I saw signs to Cedar Rapids, Iowa, 229 miles and pointed myself in that direction. I tossed my cell phone out the car window and saw it swallowed by the landscape.

I was just trying to stay out of the hands of the cops and the killers. Where are the good guys when you need them?

Chapter Eighteen

White Out

Driving into the Great Plains in January can be problematic. I worried about heading west instead of north. If I were arrested in Canada, I could escape the death penalty. The Canucks aren't keen on facilitating state sanctioned murder. I'd still likely get life but that was more like eighteen years. It would be a government run prison, as opposed to one of America's privately owned horror shows.

Despite my concerns, something deep inside me, said, stay in the U.S. and stay rural.

I saw a road sign for an I-Hop just off the expressway glowing baby blue, like a beacon in the darkness. At first, I wondered if they were open. The restaurant was as vacant as the opening scene of a zombie movie. The blonde waitress was the picture of wholesome Midwest beauty.

She smiled and turned a full 360 degrees before saying, "Take your pick,"

I ordered stuffed French toast and coffee and ate like a pig. I gave 'happy face' a generous tip because it's hard to be nice when everyone you serve seems to have a vendetta they are working on.

After filling up at an Exxon station I watched for the freeway signs, weaving through evening traffic. I knew I should pull into a motel and get some sleep, but I was amped up on caffeine and fear. I just had to drive. There was at least twenty hours of highway ahead. It made no sense to spend $60 bucks for a motel room if I was going to do nothing but toss and turn for eight hours.

It was like a bomb going off. My most brutal Death Metal playlist shocked my addled brain into wakefulness. I might go deaf but that's a worry for the future.

By the time the lights of Albert Lea came into view, I knew I had to get off the road. As though the Fates had heard me, The Stampeder Motel's illuminated sign appeared at the next off ramp.

I loved the smell of crisp fresh sheets. I inhaled deeply and felt my skin quiver.

"Fuck him! I hate him. I just need to rub one out," I murmured in the dark.

I moaned, my breath coming in short shallow gasps, my pelvis raised up to meet him. He enters me. His rigid organ ready, throbbing like a heartbeat. My body on fire I climaxed in helpless satisfaction.

I fell asleep amidst dreams of black leather, monogrammed cashmere, reckless sex, and his hungry mouth devouring the very center of my being.

194

I hated him. He shouldn't have been so nice after I slammed him in the head. He was a class act I mean until he started shooting. I was surprised that Jeremy was willing to act as his trigger man. Interesting that both Jerry and Jeremy could both be shortened to "Jer".

A sense of pleasure passed over me as the warm washcloth erased the sleep from my face. I stepped from the shower, picked up an oversized towel from the towel warmer and began drying myself. The towel quickly became a gown as I reached for another towel to dry my hair.

My hair had begun to grow out and I had bought a box of hair dye and took the time to change the color to black with bright red end tips. I liked it. I'd gone from pastel Punk to 20th century Goth overnight.

I dropped the towel and strode naked into the adjoining bedroom. I turned on the radio, filling the room with a soft rock melody.

My body moved sensually to the music, while I searched through my suitcase for a clean outfit. I decided on a white cable knit sweater and my tightest faded jeans. The change in hair color was great. I saw someone new in the mirror and I was happy about that.

Despite the change in my appearance, I felt like a train without an engineer. Moving down a track at full steam with nothing to halt the impending disaster.

It was still early, 6:45 a.m. Once I was dressed, I loaded the car with the few belongings I had taken into the room. I compulsively wiped down the room, did my systems check on the Sportage, before walking down to the motel office. I turned in my room key to the desk clerk and told her that I had vacated the room.

According to a brochure that I picked up in the motel office, I-90 was built in 1956 as part of the interstate highway system. It is the longest freeway in the United States, extending nearly 3,099 miles from Boston to Seattle. I thought that was kind of cool, until I realized that the I-90 highway is older than my Grandmother, she's only 62.

I bought a burn phone along with assorted soft drinks and sugary treats. Caffeine and carbs the fuel for my journey. I took a sip of Coke and ate a donut. My sick brain returned to Hayes and wondered where he was. Instinctively, I looked around, searching for azure eyes. My paranoia in full bloom.

I snickered, imagining him writing a check to his gazillionaire buddy to pay for the missing Kawasaki motor bike. Not that he couldn't afford it. My twisted brain imagining him explaining the circumstances.

My amusement was short-lived as I remembered all the dead bodies in the wake of my decisions. I expelled a sigh.

The little SUV was covered with dirt and road grime and the inside smelled like sweat and adrenaline. I pulled into

196

a full-service car wash and bought the Gold Package. It was nice seeing the rig clean, for a couple of minutes at least. I rectified the smell issue with an apple cinnamon air freshener I hung from the rearview mirror. My first thought was Mom's apple pie.

I did a quick scan for Hayes, coming up clear. I began to question whether that was a good thing. I desperately wanted to know where that sexy bastard was.

I looked at the map and saw I-90 from Albert Lea to Rapid City was a grueling seven and a half hours. Desperate measures would be required. Setting up the surround sound, I put "*Transylvanian Hunger*" on repeat and hit the highway. The machine gun drums, the brain crushing guitar riffs all tied together by vocals ranging from soaring heights to demonic possession. Often in the same song.

The gently rolling terrain of central Illinois and southern Michigan had melted into the flat lands of the Great Plains. Two hours west of Albert Lea I-90 was shut down due to hazardous white out conditions.

It was early afternoon when officials re-opened the highway, and we all began to move to our many separate destinations. I had lost a lot of time and from the looks of it, nothing was going to improve in the next 24-48 hours. I did a turn from the Darkthrone of the morning to The Smiths. There were times when I was convinced, I'd been born in the wrong century.

197

Since leaving Albert Lea I have been eating nothing but crap. Normally, I'm pretty health conscious. By supper time I'd downed four Cokes, three bottles of water, 6 powdered donuts, 2 frosted bear claws, a supersize box of *Good and Plenty,* and half an apple.

If I had been on my schedule, instead of beholden to Mother Nature in a sulky mood, I would have already been in Rapid City. I was still 65 miles outside Rapid City according to the last road sign.

The wind sent snow blowing into large drifts. I wasn't sure when officials considered situations hazardous, but I hadn't been able to exceed 25 miles per hour since the freeway reopened.

I was nowhere close to a restaurant meal. There were still a couple of bananas and apples in the ice chests, but I wanted something hot. I needed to find a bathroom, but I was afraid if I left the highway, they wouldn't find me until spring thaw.

I saw a Rest Area sign and to my amazement, the park had been recently plowed. Throwing my thanks to Asgard, I pulled off the freeway, parking right next to the prefab building. When I came out of the Ladies Room, I felt a sudden wave of nausea and light headedness wash over me.

I'm not sure how long I leaned against my car, acid burning the back of my throat. I was swimming for my life, through churning, crashing waves toward a swirling vortex. I blinked trying to clear the distortion. I gave an involuntary whimper, as my knees buckled. He caught me in his arms, breaking a sure face plant to the pavement fall.

I was barely conscious, in that tenuous world between gravity and zero gravity. I sensed what was happening, but it was all in slow motion. I'd lost control of my limbs. Each arm, and leg, was heavier than my limited strength to move them.

Although I couldn't focus well enough to see his face, I sensed gentle concern, both in his voice and his touch. I knew he was a westerner by his accent. Most westerners sound as if they had trained for the television news. That was my last conscious thought, that my rescuer sounded like a TV news commentator. After that, there was only blackness.

When I opened my eyes, I knew I'd passed out. I was laying on the back seat of my Sportage. Confused I wondered how he had managed to bring the back seat up with all the boxes and the Kawasaki Ninja in the way.

I had no idea how long I had been unconscious. My lapse into blackness could have been for a couple minutes, or it could have been for an hour. I knew we were still sitting in front of the bathroom at the Rest Area. I moved my head slowly from side to side, but no one was looking at me.

I was aware of another voice. It was a man's voice, an older man from the sound of him, "I don't know Luka, she's pitiful looking. She's probably a junkie. I don't think we can afford to get involved. What if she's smuggling drugs? If we get entangled with drugs we might get dumped in the middle of nowhere like that character in *"No Country for Old Men"*.

"Jesus, Dad. What are you suggesting? We just leave her here at the Rest Area to get raped, killed, or freeze to death?"

"Well, no," the older man acknowledged slowly, "but we've got to be careful. I've been reading a lot about picking up people on the road and how things turn bad. We don't want to find ourselves on the wrong end of a gun barrel."

"I know. I just don't think she's a druggie or a smuggler. I just think she's sick."

"Just look at her. She's skin and bones," the older voice exclaimed.

"Being skinny doesn't make you a drug addict."

"No, but it's usually one of the signs."

I mouthed words, hoping that I could catch hold of one. At last, I moaned, and my discomfort brought a cool cloth to my face. His face was friendly and filled with concern.

200

I often, against my own well-being, make judgments on instinct. Though all the evidence was pointing to him being one of the good guys. In this case, it seemed a reasonable conclusion. After all he had kept me from doing a nose plant and was now spending time cooling my fevered face with a damp wash cloth.

"Hi, there," he said with a grin, "I'm Luka. Luka Neilson. I'm sure glad you're a lightweight, or I wouldn't have been able to get you into your car."

"Do you want a drink of water?" he asked.

I nodded affirmatively, and he helped me raise my head so I could take several swallows of the cold liquid.

"What's your name, young lady?" Luka's Dad asked.

I licked dry lips and paused, giving me time to put my bankrupt brain in gear.

"My name is Lori. Lori Cameron, that's L-O-R-I."

"Well, hello, Lori. It's nice to meet you," he said scanning me closely, seemingly waiting for more information.

"I'm an RN. I've been volunteering at a rural clinic outside of Guadalajara, Mexico."

"Wow, a nurse. Mexico? Hmm, you look like a little kid, I wouldn't have guessed you were more than sixteen."

He nodded affirmatively, his expression unconvinced and uncommitted.

I tried to sit up, but the world began spinning and I had to put my head back down.

"I'm 23."

Lying, for me, was becoming as natural as speaking, but I was still amazed, that I could think so fast, considering my compromised physical condition.

"I'm headed to Montana. I don't think I can thank you enough for stopping to help me. I just don't know what's going on. I've been sick for several days. I think I may have picked up a bug in Mexico."

Luka stepped away from the car. I could hear him talking to someone, I assumed it was still his father.

"I don't think she's going to be able to drive. She said she's on her way to Montana. Since we're headed that way, maybe I could drive her car for a while. I can watch her, and if I need to take her to the hospital, at least she'll be only a couple hours from her destination."

"I don't know about any of this son, but I agree I wouldn't feel right about leaving her here. I'm just concerned that she might have drugs hidden in her car. I don't feel right about you driving, her rig."

"Let me see what she has to say,"

Luka returned his attention to me, and said, "Lori, we don't think you are safe to drive. My Dad and I think it would be best if I drive your car, and he follows us. We're headed to our home outside of Townsend, Montana. Where, exactly in Montana are you headed?" he asked.

"I just wanted to go to Montana. No specific destination. Just adventure seeking."

"Okay, then. Adventure coming up," he said with a gleam in his eye.

"Just try to get some sleep. Would you like a blanket?"

"A blanket would be great," I said weakly, as my body went from fever to chills, "I have blankets in a duffle bag in the cargo area."

"So, what do you think about our little plan?" he asked, spreading a pink blanket across me, tucking it under my chin and then around my body.

I liked the feel of his hands touching me. He was ruggedly handsome, his hair white, blonde. The image of fitness and Norwegian good health.

"Whatever you think, is great with me," I mumbled.

As sick and dizzy as I felt, I had a sense that I would be much safer with Luka and his father. There's no shame in taking a hand when it's offered, especially if you need it, I convinced myself.

"Thank you so much. I can't tell you how much I appreciate your help. I think you're right. I don't think I can drive, and I'm definitely afraid to spend the night here or on the roadside," I said, visibly grimacing.

"The way things are going, road conditions being what they are, we are at least two hours out of Rapid City. Just close your eyes and try to get some sleep.

"I guess I'm in no position to put up a fight," I said with fabricated resignation.

"Glad to hear it. I probably outweigh you by 125 pounds," implying that he could take me out.

"I have seven years of kick boxing experience. I'm a competitor," I stated proudly, "It is all about how you use your weight."

I watched his quickly camouflaged smirk, "Yes, Ma'am."

After a short pause, his face close enough that his warm cinnamon scented breath tickled my skin, close enough to kiss me, he said, "Shh. Get some rest."

204

It must be the looming prospect of the death sentence that has sent my sex hormones into overdrive. Or, perhaps, my recent three weeks with a slave master was the explanation. Whatever the reason I wished Luka would kiss me and just hold me. I hoped he didn't recognize the sexual yearning in my eyes, as I felt unable to conceal the extent of my arousal.

Luka climbed behind the wheel of my Sportage and continued my playlist. With my favorite easy listening tunes playing, and the rocking motion of the vehicle, I found myself sliding inexorably toward sleep within just minutes of leaving the Rest Area.

I heard muffled voices and opened my eyes to the bright canopy lights of a Stop 'N Go gas station. I struggled in my blanket cocoon to peer over the front seat.

Luka was under the hood of my rig talking to the service attendant.

"Check the anti-freeze and the oil, would you, please?" I heard him say.

I felt my brow wrinkle. I hadn't checked either of those recently. I crossed my fingers and bit my lip. I could see Luka wiping his hands with a towel supplied by the attendant.

When I caught his eye, he walked up to the car window.

"No real concerns, but you were a little low on a couple things. The attendant is bringing them up to recommended levels."

"I've had a lot on my mind. I guess I need to be more careful about such things," I said with obvious anxiety, looking down at my knotted fingers.

"Hey," he twisted his neck and bent down peering in my window, "Nothing bad happened. It's taken care of, now. Okay?" Changing the subject adroitly, "They have a little deli. Want something? I think you should eat."

"I need to use the bathroom," I said, looking toward the little clapboard building.

He opened the car door and watched as I untangled my long legs from the confines of the back seat. As I stood, my legs wobbled noticeably. Thankfully, he reached out and helped steady me.

"Just call me Jell-O legs," I said with a self-deprecating laugh.

I ducked my head to conceal a surge of heat that warmed my cheeks.

"Let me help," he said, while extending his arm to offer support.

"I'm good."

"No, you need help. The bathroom is just inside the door," he said taking my arm, the crease between his eyebrows deepening.

I allowed him to help me. The wind snapped at our clothes. The gusts resisted our push across the fuel lane, forcing us to fight for traction as we struggled to the shelter of the building.

Fugitives get used to throwing up in sinks and toilets. Fear twists your thinking and your digestive track. Nausea has become my near constant companion.

It was like a light went off in my brain. I suddenly worried, could I be pregnant? Every pregnant woman I ever heard of threw up her guts the first three months. I had been without birth control while I was with Hayes. I put a hand to my belly and hoped not. Would Hayes take the baby while I served my life term? I tried to imagine him the loving involved father. I hoped we would never find out.

I opened the bathroom door and paused at the threshold, judging the distance from the bathroom to the exit door. I took several long, slow deep breaths, straightened up, and walked up to Luka who was leaning against the cashier's counter.

I grabbed a package of cinnamon gun from the display next to me. Just as he turned to look at me, I extended the package of gum in his direction.

He squinted and said, "You should try to eat something."

Confused, I looked around at the display of packaged chemicals cramming the Stop 'N Go's shelves, twisted my mouth and ran my tongue on my lip before I said, "I'm mostly vegan. Maybe a package of crackers might help my stomach."

"Do you have any crackers?" Luka asked the wizened cashier.

"Yes, sir," he pointed his index finger toward a spot at the back of the store.

Luka jogged off, returning in a minute with several packages of crackers and cheese. He paid for the crackers and the cinnamon chewing gum, took my arm, and guided me toward the front door.

We were nearly blown back to the car, by whipping gusts of wind. Back at the rig, Luka opened the back door for me. I resisted climbing in.

"Could I sit up front, with you?"

"Are you sure? It might be better for you to stay in the back where you can lay down."

"No, no, please," I moaned, taking him by the arm and giving him my most martyred expression.

208

"Well, okay, but I'm going to have to move a few things around. Why don't you sit in the driver's seat for a few minutes while I reorganize?"

"Okay," I said, as he helped me into the driver's seat.

My Nordic god, my Viking lord.

I ran my hands haphazardly thru my hair, knowing the resulting chaos would not improve my distressed appearance. I took two packages of crackers and the gum from his extended hand. My heart skipped a beat. The air was electric.

I watched Luka lower the back seat, creating more cargo space. He quickly reorganized, moving a bunch of my stuff from the front passenger seat to the back.

When he reached for the two long guns, still covered by a blanket I said, "Careful, they're loaded."

"Thanks for the warning."

With the front passenger seat cleared, Luka leaned across the front seat and asked, "What should I do with your purse?"

"Just leave it on the floor up there," I said, watching him continue to work.

"How did you make room to get the back seat up," I asked as casually as I could manage,"

209

"It wasn't easy, but I was an Eagle Scout and I'm used to doing the impossible," he laughed.

For the first time, I noticed a newer blue van parked behind the Sportage. It must be Luka's vehicle. There was a handsome mustachioed man, wearing a red and black plaid winter jacket and a big ass cowboy hat in the driver's seat. Finally, I could put a face to Luka's father.

I was surprised to see several other people in the van. Sitting in the front passenger seat was a beautiful woman with long blonde hair. Luka's Mother I assumed. Behind her I could see two other blonde heads, but I could not tell more than that.

Luka had me take his arm as we walked around the car to the passenger seat, helped me into the car and fastened my seat belt.

"I'm sorry, I still can't believe you're twenty-three, and a Registered Nurse," he said, so close I felt his warm breath on my cheek.

"Do you want to see my driver's license?"

"No, that's alright. You just look so young. You act so young."

His eyes were an eerie amber, an eye color I had truly never seen before.

"Lots of people say that. I think it's this stupid haircut," I said pulling my fingers through my hair.

"Hmmm, maybe," he said softly, holding my eyes with his, changing the topic he asked, "Did you eat those crackers?"

"Yes, sir. Thank you."

"Did they help?"

"I think so."

He didn't believe me. I could see it in his strange amber eyes. He knew I was lying. He knew I wasn't twenty-three. He assumes that I am not an RN. He's probably wondering why I have such a well-developed and elaborate story. He's probably thinking his father was right, I'm a druggie or a mule. I bit my lip and waited, but he said nothing more.

He was big boned, with well-developed muscles that went with his commanding height. He was big enough to make me feel petite, which was no small feat.

I was convinced that Luka wouldn't be so nice if he figured out who I was. Thankfully, there was no reason to expect that he ever would. Our connection was destined to be short.

Without further comment, he walked back to the van and had a short conversation with his Dad, before coming back and climbing behind the wheel of the Sportage.

I was glad Luka was driving. I did not want to be behind the wheel. I hoped my fainting episode might prove fortuitous. He talked while I mostly listened, for which I was extremely thankful.

At some point we crossed the Wyoming border heading west. I was feeling more relaxed and less sick. Both good things. The storm was moving east, and I was happy to see it depart.

Luka questioned me about my plans. I elaborated on my volunteer stint in Mexico. I told him how glad I was to be back in the good old USA. I hoped my brief responses would be enough, but my answers didn't satisfy him. He wanted to know all about me. I didn't understand his curiosity. He wanted to know about my family, my childhood, my home, my job, where I had gotten my nursing degree. What was I supposed to do, tell him the truth?

I had Aunt Janet's information to answer many of his questions. I hated lying. It is so damn hard to keep track of what you told, to who. I'd noticed that each time you challenge your moral compass, stretching its perfect original shape to some new twisted form, it was impossible for it to ever return to its original perfection.

I told as few lies as I could. Under the circumstances that was difficult. I told him that my parents lived in Seattle. I admitted to being unemployed. I volunteered that I had little money and was living on a shoestring, ignoring the fact that between my parka and my little safe I had stashed over $25,000 in cash.

I told him I planned to be a Travel Nurse, which would allow me to take short term contracts at different hospitals around the country. In fact, I told him I had decided that nursing wasn't for me and that as soon as I could I wanted to leave nursing for a career as a writer.

"Please don't take offense, but how could you possibly have lived enough to have something to write about?"

"If I could only tell you," I said.

I turned away, focusing on the darkness of the Wyoming night.

"Well, be sure to let me read the first draft of that novel," he said with a somber look.

I said nothing more and hoped the subject of my life history would end there, but I suspected it wouldn't.

Chapter Nineteen

Harvard Law

Luka seemed to have no secrets. He talked openly about his family, his college life, and his dreams. He had graduated from Harvard Law four years before and was a partner in a large Helena law firm in addition to being a participating manager of his family's various business ventures.

Sometimes in life, people just click. Sometimes a relationship feels as comfortable as your favorite pair of jeans. That's the way I felt about Luka.

He had been engaged for two years to another law student. In the end, they decided to call it off. She was from New York and the last thing she wanted to do was spend her life in Montana. He'd been single since the breakup.

I told him a little bit about Mateo and that we weren't together anymore. I didn't elaborate, other than to say what a great person he was and that I'd thought I loved him.

Luka could be funny, he could be serious, he was smart, and fucking sexy as hell. As we drove, he told me he wanted me to see where he grew up. He told me he had grown up in a log cabin on a wilderness mountaintop.

"It is the most beautiful spot in the world, you can touch the sky, every day."

I smiled.

"You could write. We could ride horses, chase the dog. We could, play, house."

I let the comment settle.

"W-w-what? I stuttered stupidly.

"I said that wrong," he said awkwardly with a short laugh, "I just want you to see our place. There's a peace and tranquility there that you will never find anywhere else, no matter where you wander in this wide world," he said, his voice quieting, his eyes distant.

Six months ago, I was just a high school kid, headed to Yale on a basketball scholarship. I was still a virgin who had had only one sorta' boyfriend in my whole life. After six months on the run, my sorta boyfriend was dead, I had been deflowered by a magazine handsome cop and had then been held captive for nineteen days by a richer than Midas slave master. I was feeling a sexual maturity that I would never have expected or imagined just a few short months ago.

I told Luka I was intrigued by the invitation, but I wanted time to think about it. The thought of horseback riding the open prairie and the pine forests of Montana sounded intoxicating. I thought Luka was intoxicating.

215

I needed a safe, buffered place. At least temporarily. A place where I could relax and regenerate.

Lives had been cut short and I was now the only person left to tell the story. The story of Ward, Cory, and Sky. An out of the way ranch in Montana might be the perfect place to hunker down for a while.

I don't know when we crossed the Montana border. It was still dark when I woke up, but I could tell daybreak was not far away. I heard Luka talking to someone, and I rubbed my eyes and sat up just as we were pulling away from an AMPM gas station.

"Where are we," I asked sleepily.

"Somewhere south of where I want to be," he said with a smirk.

"Funny. But where exactly is that?" I asked.

"We're in Hastings, a small town thirty miles from the house," he answered.

"I'm getting muscle cramps," I complained irritably.

"You're complaining? I've been driving for fourteen straight hours."

His complaint was not lost on me, and I imagined he must be exhausted. We were now following the blue van. After a short drive, we came to a large wrought iron gate

216

blocking the roadway. In an arched frame above the gate were the words *"Grizzly Ranch."*

We were at least two miles down the gravel road when I saw the sun breaking over a ridge of mountains. Finally, as we cleared the trees, I saw a massive log structure that resembled a hunting lodge. It looked like a fucking movie set.

The road split. The road we were on swung into a large circular driveway. Within seconds of shutting off the car engine two men in boots and cowboy hats hurried down the front steps and began helping to unload the van.

"Welcome home folks," the two men chorused.

Mr. Neilson appeared much larger in his familiar surroundings.

"Brad. Jesse. We're damn glad to be home!"

I wasn't sure what to do, so I sat waiting for instructions. Luka climbed out of the Sportage and walked over to where his family was clustered. There was an abbreviated conversation amongst them before Luka walked back to me.

"Maybe I should go thank them or something," I said.

"You'll see them again. You're invited to the house for dinner tonight, but right now I want to help you get settled."

"Settled?" I asked my eyes searching his.

"Yeah, I thought you were going to stay for a while?"

"I don't remember telling you I was coming home with you," I said slowly.

I wasn't a lost puppy after all.

"I don't remember you saying no," he responded, giving me a quick wink.

The wink reminded me of Hayes, causing my hands to shake.

"I was sleeping on it," I said, hoping it sounded better out loud.

"Well, we're here now.

"I guess that means, I'm here for at least a couple of days," I said with a cautious smile.

"Well, it's settled then," he laughed, "Let me show you your temporary digs."

"Okay," I said, wiping away a rogue tear that had escaped the corner of my eye.

"Hey, what's this all about?" we don't allow tears here, at least not on the first day."

"I'm sorry. I've had a harrowing, last few months."

"Well, that's a shame. I'm truly, sorry," he said, squeezing my hand.

That first vanquished teardrop was quickly joined by a cavalcade of clones and I tried to wipe them away with the back of my hand, but the tears were coming too fast.

"Is there something you need to talk about?"

"No, why would you ask something like that?" my mouth a rigid line, my shoulders hunched down, my mind a black pit. I hated appearing so weak.

He reached across my lap and once again took my hand, and this time just held it. I did not protest. I appreciated a hand to hold on to. I said nothing more, but instead stared out the car window at the beauty of a Montana sunrise, watching shafts of light awaken a dark and shadowed landscape.

The gravel road was narrow and snaked through a forest of yellow and jack pines climbing to a broad ridge top where it emerged in front of a beautiful log home surrounded by unending sky. I gasped and saw him glance at me.

"Let's get you to bed."

219

I wasn't sure whether he expected to join me in bed, but I decided to see where this encounter was headed.

Luka fished a key from his pants pocket and opened the front door. When it swung open a wall of windows view welcomed us.

He took my hand and walked me to a set of French doors next to the fireplace and swung them open together in one swift action. Luka led me out onto the expansive deck that ran across the back of the cabin. He took hold of the lodge pole pine railing and breathed deeply.

"I love this place. I was conceived here," he turned toward me with a crooked grin, "In fact, I spent the first ten years of my life in this house."

"You are amazingly fortunate," I said as I looked over the expanse of sky and golden plains.

"I've heard the phrase, 'Big Sky Country' but until this moment, I never understood what it meant. Please, tell me about this place."

"My Mother was a Monroe. She was from a wealthy old Montana family. Her grandparents came to Montana by covered wagon. She thought like my Father. They'd grown up together. Her parents owned vast land tracts, one of which, is the piece we are standing on."

He stretched and yawned. His eyelids were hanging at half-mast. A blonde stubble shadowed his face and I wanted to feel that stubble against my skin.

"I'm tired," he said.

"It's okay, you can tell me about this place some other time."

He ignored me, continuing,

"So, after my Father proposed, he asked Mom where she wanted to live after they were married. She brought him up here. Her parents gave them this land, and my Dad, with several local craftsmen, set about building this house. My parents moved in here on their wedding day."

"That is so romantic,"

"Is it?" he asked quietly.

Luka turned and gazed at me before touching my face. My heart was slamming recklessly into my chest wall, and my next breath was hung up somewhere between my feet and my panties.

He took my face in his two hands, and just stared at me.

"It may be too soon, in fact, I'm convinced it is, but I need to tell you that I'm feeling something special toward you. I'm finding myself attracted to you on multiple levels."

221

He looked away from my face, seemingly searching the distant mountains for the right words.

"I'm hoping with time, I'll figure out what it is that has hypnotized me," his eyes drawn back toward me, he sucked in a breath, "I know we met less than 24 hours ago, but I knew I couldn't just let you drive away. I had to bring you here, to a place I love more than should be allowed."

I had no response, and I just let him talk.

"I think it is only fair, to tell you, my testosterone is raging nearly out of control. I want to take some time and find out if it's simple lust, or there's a deeper emotional connection. How do you feel about that?"

He gently kissed my hair, and then both cheeks. I heard myself breathe heavily just before he kissed me on the lips and wrapped me in his arms.

I wasn't sure if it was lust or a deeper bond either, but I thought I wanted to explore the possibilities. I was frightened by the passion of my own feelings and what Luka might be expecting from our embryonic relationship.

He released his embrace and extended me to arm's length and looked me up and down.

"I don't want to leave you alone, but I'm beat. I've got to get some sleep."

I knew he was right. Sleep was what both of us needed.

"The cabin is always ready for company. Foodwise it's canned and packaged goods until we can get to a store. The well water is fantastic. I suggest you take a shower, get some sleep. I'll come pick you up for dinner at 6:00.

"What should I wear? I've spent the last year in Mexico. I have a great shorts and T's collection, but that's about all."

"Denim, flannel, and boots," a smirk tugged at the corner of his mouth.

"I can pull something together then," I said with restored confidence.

"I've got to say goodbye before I pass out on your couch. If it's okay, I'm going to borrow your car to get me back to the house. If you need anything, just pick up the phone and dial 99, that will connect you to someone in the main house."

He bent down, tipped my chin up and kissed me gently on the lips.

"Let's get the last of your bags inside, so you can get organized, and I can get on my way."

I helped Luka unload all my belongings from the car and got them inside the cabin. As he walked into the yard ready to leave, I chased after him. I caught him next to the Sportage, throwing him off balance when I grabbed him by the arm, turning him around to face me.

"I like you too," I said, "I want to find out where we can take this thing, we are both feeling."

"Good," he laughed as he climbed behind the wheel of my rig.

I gave a small wave, bit my lip, and watched until the little SUV rounded the corner and disappeared down the hill.

Chapter Twenty

Just Family

Luka was holding my hand when we stepped into the massive entry hall at the main house. From the entry hall you could see through the living room to the infinity pool and a wilderness lake beyond.

"Hello!" Luka hollered, "We're here!"

"We're in the family room. Come join us," I heard a male voice answer back.

"Do I look okay?" I whispered, rotating in front of him in my faded flannel shirt, jeans, and denim vest.

"You couldn't look bad."

He slid his arm around my shoulder, effectively guiding me toward an area at the back of the house. Vaulted ceilings soared to the stratosphere, a massive, exposed stone fireplace dominated the room. A blazing fire welcomed us. I quickly realized all eyes were on me.

"Hi," I said looking from face to face, "I'm Lori."

"Let me make some introductions," Luka suggested.

"We gotta' set of twins here, Kyle and Josie."

225

He did a mock wrestling move and grabbed a handsome high schooler around the chest.

"This ugly guy is my brother Kyle. Kyle this is my friend, Lori. Shake her hand."

Kyle twisted from Luka's grasp and stuck out his hand and I shook it ritualistically, three solid pumps.

Luka grabbed a teenage girl with white, blonde hair and the same incredible amber eyes that Luka had been blessed with, by the hand, and pulled her in my direction.

"This spoiled, but incredibly beautiful young lady, is my sister, Josie. Josie this is Lori. Give her a hug."

"Luka likes telling everybody what to do. He wouldn't get away with it if he weren't so damn good looking," Josie said using her hand to push on his chest.

We meshed in an awkward, but good natured, embrace.

"And this cranky old guy is my Dad, Kent Neilson. Dad this is Lori. Give her a hug.

Mr. Neilson was less awkward than Josie, and we embraced easily. Close-up, without his hat, I realized Mr. Neilson was an elder version of his son.

"I like to save the best for the last, this is my mother, Isabell. Come here Isabell. This woman is our rock," he smiled and kissed her on the cheek.

"Isabell this is Lori. You know what to do," he joked.

"He told me you were beautiful," she said, as she hugged me for several extended seconds.

Quite frankly, Isabell was the most beautiful woman I had ever seen, and I had to lower my eyes to keep from openly gawking.

"Well now that we are all friends, let's get the food on the table," Mr. Neilson said, followed by an infectious laugh, with us all joining in.

It was just after 10:00 when Luka pulled the SUV up in front of the cabin.

"They loved you," he said.

"I loved them too," I answered, matching the intensity of his gaze.

"Do you want to come in?" I asked.

"Of course, I want to come in," he said with a grin.

The ghost of a smile haunted the corners of my mouth. We walked across the driveway arm-in-arm and into the cabin.

He closed the door and leaned with his back against it. Still holding my hand, he pulled me close. With the touch of his index finger, he raised my chin, leaving me unable to do anything but stare into those amber eyes.

Luka swallowed me with his arms, pulling me tight against him. His mouth against mine, his teeth nibbling and pulling at my lips, teasing me with his tongue, playing a game of, 'catch me, if you can'.

I hesitantly ran my fingertips across his cheek. Luka leaned into my touch and closed his eyes, expelling a breath of air. His fingers began an invasive exploration of my mouth. I'm feeling a growing sexual intensity.

He opened his eyes and I hear him growl sensually from deep in his diaphragm.

He stepped back, pulled his cell phone from his pocket, found a Soft Sounds play list before setting the phone on the kitchen island.

"I like to dance. How about you?"

"I love to dance," I said taking his hand.

He took me in his arms, and we melted together for "Here Without You," followed by "I'll Be There for You."

I felt heaven was just a couple songs away.

"Are you hungry?"

"We just ate a couple hours ago."

"I'm kind of into late night snacks," he said his face buried in my hair.

"I think I saw a box of mac & cheese."

"I thought you were vegan?"

"Mostly vegan. And I didn't say I was hungry," I giggled.

"Give me a second and I'll see what I can find."

I headed to the kitchen, while he sat at the island. I looked through the cabinets, and quickly found the box of pasta and cheese heart attack. I could sense his eyes focused on my ass, and I fucking loved it.

I located a pot and in a few minutes the mac and cheese was ready.

"Not going to have any?" he asked.

"After I looked at the ingredients, I remembered why I'm a vegan," I said simply, "In fact you probably shouldn't eat that stuff either. I think it is bio-hazardous."

"I'll take my chances," he said.

"I think I'll have an apple."

"Good luck," Luka winked.

229

"With what?"

"Pesticides. Fruit is covered with them."

I washed the McIntosh in the sink before taking a bite.

"How big is *"Grizzly Ranch?"* I asked, searching for a topic about him.

He took a swallow of his ice water tabbed his mouth with the makeshift napkin before answering.

"960,000 plus acres."

I felt my eyes blink as I tried to envision '960,000 plus acres' on a map. I said nothing and he continued.

"It is the largest privately owned ranch in Montana, and one of the largest contiguously owned properties in the United States. It stretches across half of central and eastern Montana a big chunk of northern Wyoming, and a section in both North and South Dakota."

I was used to the large expanses of wilderness and prairie land of eastern Oregon, mostly BLM land. But I couldn't even process the size of the '*Grizzly Ranch*'.

Lake Oswego, Oregon, my hometown is an enclave for the mostly well-to-do on a beautiful lake just outside Portland. So, my concept of large land holdings has been influenced by my limited experience.

The immensity of such a parcel was unimaginable to me. I presumed that his father was extraordinarily wealthy and presumably wielded immense political power across four states. My knowledge of Montana was limited to the fact that it was close to Canada.

"One of my Dad's goals is to increase the 'Grizzly' to over a million contiguous acres. The ranch is already well over 960,000 acres, but I haven't added up several recent small purchases. In fact, we may already have reached his goal."

"How does someone acquire nearly a million acres?" I asked, trying to mask my astonishment.

Some folks are more fortunate than others. Others are more hardworking. My family is both hardworking and lucky."

"I see. Give me a little history. I'm curious. Unless you don't want to talk about your family."

"I love to talk about my family. As I told you, my Mother was a Monroe. The property belonged to her family. They gave this property to my parents for a wedding present."

"Beats the hell out of a toaster," I snickered.

He smirked and continued eating mac & cheese between sentences.

"The Neilson's were even more wealthy than the Monroe's. They came to Montana in the 1830's and built an empire on gold, silver and timber."

"Got any more?" Luka asked, indicating the empty mac & cheese bowl.

"My Father was born rich. When he was six, he inherited 375,000 acres from his paternal grandfather, along with millions of dollars in stock, plus another $100,000,000 in oil and gas leases," he said talking easily without reservation or hesitation.

He looked around the cabin, his eyes pausing several times, before, moving on.

"In those days, when we lived here with my Mother, he was young and wild and believed in living off the land. Maybe, because he'd always had money, it didn't affect his thinking, or his lifestyle. I guess you could call him the original survivalist. I remember, we usually fished, or hunted for our dinner. He'd always say, "if we don't catch a fish, we won't eat.""

I laughed.

"Well, if you are wondering, we never missed a meal. Of course, I don't remember ever coming home without a fish, a squirrel, a coon, or a deer, either."

He took his bowl and silverware to the sink and rinsed it out. I was surprised at how easily he talked about himself, his family, and their vast wealth.

"My Mom and Dad believed that happiness comes from love of family and love of the land. It may sound crazy, but my Dad is a very frugal man. He believes man has been given everything he needs to live a good life. Above everything else, my Father is a man of the land, a man, in the true Montana spirit, in the Indian way."

We had spent the night, just talking and dancing, "The sun is coming up," I said, "Let's go outside."

"We'll need coats," Luka said, looking around.

"Here we go," I said, getting our coats and gloves from the closet.

We stepped out onto the deck and I felt my heart surge with happiness as he comfortably slid his arm around my shoulder and held me close. Together we looked to the spectacular vista and watched an eagle float lazily on an early morning air current.

"I forgot to tell you, I put the Kawasaki Ninja in the loafing shed. I noticed it had Illinois plates."

Leaving me to explain, why I had an expensive sport bike with Illinois plates.

I had totally spaced out the Kawasaki sport bike from Winnetka, "I lived at a house in Middletown, Illinois for a couple months, after coming back from Mexico. I had a deal with the owner to clean up the place in exchange for free rent. I got to keep or sell anything on the property."

"I want to make sure I have this right. In your short life you have earned a nursing degree, become a semi-pro kickboxer, and are a motor cross rider? Anything else you want to tell me, Ms. athlete extraordinaire?"

"I'm a fuckin' hot skier and I used to be pretty good at H-O-R-S-E and Knockout," I bragged.

"Well, you've come to the right place. We're a basketball family. We've got a court down at the main house. Maybe one of these days when we get a crowd together, we'll do a team challenge. I think Kyle and Josie would give you a run for your money. Those two are real hotshots. Both got great scholarship offers. Kyle is headed to Duke and Josie has decided on USC."

Sweet Zeus. Why did I bring up basketball? Luka had me so relaxed it just fell out of my unbridled mouth.

"I also found something else when I unloaded your rig," his tone notably darker.

I looked away from his face and swallowed, waiting for him to tell me what he had found.

234

"In addition to the loaded long guns I found a loaded semi-automatic handgun hidden under the front seat."

"An unloaded gun isn't worth much. I'm a woman traveling alone. I'm good at kick boxing but nothing tops a gun for serious situations."

"Right you are. What about the long guns?"

"I grew up hunting. I'd feel naked without my rifle and shotgun," I said, semi-truthfully.

"The woman of my dreams," he confirmed, before adding, "I'm going to head back to the main house. I've got to get some sleep. I suggest you do the same."

He took me in his arms and lifted me off the ground and swung me around a couple times. He put me down and leaned against me pushing me against one of the support beams and kissed me aggressively.

Soon we were all tongues, lips, and hickeys. We became more heated and he moved on to second base and I held on tight. I thought he was going to close the seduction when he began to caress my crotch through my jeans, but he held back and after what seemed like an eternity, finally backed away.

"Good night."

"Good night," I echoed.

235

Chapter Twenty One

Starting Again

My relationship with Luka was verging on weird. We were involved in a bizarre dating ritual where we would arouse one another to near insanity and stop just short of intercourse. We both wanted to see if there was something more between us than just mind-bending lust.

Well, it had become a crude joke and I don't think it was good for either one of us. Anyway, that was the craziness we had created for ourselves. Truthfully, I'm not sure if it was more me or Luka. For my part, I had collected a lot of baggage.

Luka spent most weekdays at his house in Helena. His law practice kept him busy, with private clients and family projects, including legislative issues related to family interests. He came home to the 'Grizzly' every Friday afternoon by noon and didn't leave for Helena until Monday about noon.

We spent a lot of time together. Mostly we did outdoor things. We both loved fishing, hiking, motor biking, kayaking, or just panning for gold out on the Warm Springs Creek. He had become over a short time a treasured friend. He always stayed at the main house, but our evenings were often late. Our life was quiet and uncomplicated.

237

As for relieving our sexual frustrations there was a lot of masturbation and vibrator use on my part and, I'm guessing, a lot of stroking on Luka's part.

I was frugal with my money and the Neilson's refused to let me pay rent. I had the small safe but rarely opened it. I wanted a cushion in case I might have to make an unscheduled run for it. With that in mind I figured it wouldn't hurt to make a few extra bucks.

I unpacked my jewelry making supplies and organized them in bins. Luka helped by bringing an old work bench from the basement of the main house up to the cabin and I was ready to go in business.

"Not so fast, sweetie. If you are going to do this, I want you protected legally. I'm going to draw up incorporation documents and take care of your tax filings."

As Luka promised, becoming a corporation was no big deal. He took care of everything. Who said there were too many regulations limiting the aspiring entrepreneur?

I took some great photos of my jewelry stock and made up a sales catalogue, much like what I had used in Chicago and showed it to Luka. He took it, showed it both to Isabell and Josie, and I had my first sales in Montana, as "Rescued Jewels".

I opened the door to a knock and found Isabell standing fresh and smiling, her blonde hair tied high on her head in a ponytail. She stepped across the threshold and I gave her a quick hug.

She laughed, before saying she had stopped by "on business."

"I hope you don't get upset, but Josie and I liked your jewelry collection so much we took the liberty to make copies of your catalogue and passed it around to our friends and mailed it to a few specialty retailers we often buy from."

"Really? Well, thank you."

She pulled a bank money bag from her jacket pocket.

"What's this?"

"Everyone was so excited with your collection that they wanted to buy something. In fact, they have ordered a ton of merchandize. I have here checks, and cash and paperwork for the orders."

"I-I-I don't know what to say, other than thank you."

"I'm not done yet, honey. I have collected three boxes of old costume jewelry from friends to help you fuel your business. Can you give me a hand bringing it in?"

"We'll just put it in the spare bedroom. Better known as my workshop."

"Want some coffee or tea?" I asked when we were done.

She pulled her handheld from her jacket pocket and verified the time, "I'll have to take a rain check. Anna is off on Sundays and Mondays, so I need to go home and get something pulled together for dinner. We'll plan lunch or something, though. Okay?"

"Thanks again for everything," I said motioning broadly with my arms.

"Holy smokes, I nearly forgot. Josie wanted me to tell you that she thinks you should forget the Sunday Market idea and focus on selling your jewelry at select high-end boutiques in tourist destinations such as Sun Valley, Aspen, Coronado, and Santa Barbara. She's made up a contact list for you with addresses and phone numbers. The list is in the bank bag with the orders."

"Kiss her for me," I said, a bit overwhelmed.

"Josie has been on the phone making some contacts for you. Her best friend's Mother has a part interest in specialty shops in Aspen, Yellowstone and Breckenridge."

I'm going crazy. I mean I am going fucking crazy. How did me talking about making some recycled bracelets and selling them at the Sunday Market, translate into corporate meetings, and rich clients?

240

I stood awkwardly at the door, trying to harness the right words.

"It's hard for me to be a one-woman show. I really mean it. I am thankful for every bit of help you and Josie have given me. And now all your friends. I am so grateful, but I have some limits. I'm only one person."

Isabell seemed not to hear me.

"Hug time," she instructed.

We embraced and then she turned and dashed like a deer across the yard and climbed into her truck. I watched as she maneuvered the big red Dodge pickup around my Sportage and headed back down the road to the main house.

I felt a tear threaten to break the eyelash barrier. The challenge of having so many supportive loving people within arm's reach, was sometimes more than my damaged psyche could deal with.

Suddenly I felt marooned without a compass. I knew I would need to leave, soon, but it would require a bit more planning than I had used in the past. I didn't want to hurt Luka or his family.

I called time-out and went courtside for a bottle of water. and wiped the sweat off my face with my bare forearm.

It was Luka, me, Isabell, the two ranch hands Brad and Jesse, facing off against Josie, Kyle, Kent, Anna the housekeeper and another ranch hand named Hondo. Kyle and Josie were basketball dynamos, both having scholarship offers. Each was tall with great raw talent.

Josie was the more serious foe while Kyle liked to showboat. I loved his hot dogging and thought of the many times I had pulled similar stunts to irritate and agitate the other team. I imagined him in a real game, he had star written all over him. I had forgotten how much I missed the game.

"Anytime you old folks are ready to play, the "A Team" here, is ready to kick ass," Kyle hooted in my direction.

I shook off the insult. I was not going to let him goad me into showing my stuff.

"Just be cool, look cool," I whispered to myself.

I played like I had no real ability. When the makeshift time clock blared, Kyle's team had beat us by 15 points.

"Good game," Kyle said throwing his arms around me and Luka, "We used to do this a couple times a week," he said. You need to come down from the mountaintop more often, and I'll teach you how to play the game."

"Okay," I laughed.

242

"Lori, did you play any sports in high school or college?" he asked.

"I was into kickboxing."

"Wow. I'll watch myself," Kyle teased.

"Where did you go to school?" he asked.

"Annie Wright's, Tacoma, Washington, class of 2014," I said easily.

"Annie Wright's? That's kind of a strange name."

"It's a boarding school," I said uneasily.

"Really? Boarding school? That sounds European," he said seemingly amused.

"My parent's thought I needed a bit of fine tuning," I giggled.

"What about college?"

"I went to nursing school," I answered, desperate to stop his questions.

"Which one?" he continued his seemingly endless probing.

"OHSU, Portland, Oregon."

The conversation was starting to make me nervous. Kyle could pull up the yearbook online and find out I was lying about going to school at Annie Wright's. And the OHSU answer, was just pitiful. For God sakes couldn't I have come up with something a bit further away from Lake Oswego than OHSU?

Once Kyle knew I was lying about Annie Wright's, he would probably go to the OHSU website and investigate that claim. Once he knew I had lied about both high school and college, I suspected Kyle's curiosity would be sent into overdrive and he'd be on the phone to Luka.

Every lie is like stepping in a quicksand pit. Every lie as dangerous, as telling the truth, and consequently, both as dangerous as the other.

"Hey Luka, I was thinking I wanted you to come by for dinner. What do you say?" I asked him when we reached the parking area. "Not the whole gang, just you."

"You couldn't keep me away," Luka said, taking my hand as we walked to the Sportage, "Remember, I've had your mac & cheese."

"I need to get to the supermarket. You feel like tagging along?" I asked.

"I'd like to do that. You want to go now?"

"That would be awesome."

244

Luka had promised to "bring the best steaks in the world," produced right on the *Grizzly* range, when he came by at 7:00. I had already made up a loaf of cheese bread, a big bowl of salad, and iced the Pellegrino. When we were at the supermarket, Luka had snagged a chocolate cake for dessert. I was ready and waiting when I heard the rap on the door.

Luka opened the cabin door just as my hand touched the doorknob.

"Hi, babe," he said and kissed me on the cheek and presented me with a bouquet of red roses and white carnations.

"Wow, flowers and steaks, things don't get much better than this," I said joyfully.

Taking the flowers from his hand I told him, "I'm going to get these in water."

"Everything else is ready we just need to throw the cheese bread in the oven for a couple minutes before the steaks are done," I said, looking over my shoulder at him, "The flowers are beautiful. Thank you."

"How do you want to do the steaks?" Luka queried.

"I've got the broiler heating up. Open up the package and throw a little salt, pepper and minced garlic on the steaks and we'll get them under the broiler."

"Sounds perfect."

"How about some music?" I asked.

"I'm on it," he promised.

"I'll finish the steaks," I offered.

I placed the flowers on the counter and watched Luka as he fiddled with his playlist. He was deliciously handsome, looking healthy and sexy in perfectly fitting well-worn jeans and a red and gray Pendleton plaid shirt over a white T with hand tooled belt and fine hand-crafted Mexican boots.

While I stood at the sink, he came up behind me and wrapped his arms over my shoulders and both hands found my breasts and slowly teased the nipples through my shirt. I turned around in his embrace and felt my nostrils flare and my cheeks flush.

Our kisses were deep and demanding. My hand found his groin and I rub the hardened cock through his jeans.

He deposited small pecks across my cheeks and ran his fingertips up and down my neck and behind my ear. Everything was perfect.

I wrestled my eyes from his face and reinvested my interest in the top rivet of his jeans. I exhaled and tensed my vagina, squeezing rhythmically as I opened each rivet from top to bottom. I slid my hand into the opening and touched his erection through his shorts.

246

He backed away, dropped his jeans and I dropped to my knees, took his dick in my mouth, and sucked him until he came in a flood of thick cum.

It was approaching midnight. After tamping down an explosion of heated sexual intensity we shifted gears and watched a movie, talked about my growing jewelry business, the Neilson family, their life on the *'Grizzly Ranch'*, music, Spring Salmon, and a partridge in a pear tree. Then I ventured on to a topic that I wasn't sure if I should broach, but I took the step.

"You said your Mother was killed in a car accident?

"I said that didn't I."

"Yes, you said that. Don't feel as if you are required to talk about her if you don't want to."

"I know that. I talk to you because I want to. I don't share with many people."

"You barely know me."

"Sometimes, you don't need to know someone well, to know their heart."

I nodded, took his hand, and deposited a series of baby kisses on its back.

Without any further comment on our growing bond, he switched gears back to his Mother.

"She was coming back from a memorial service in Helena. The weather was terrible. Subsequent reports, called it white out conditions."

He stopped talking. I watched his brow pucker. I could tell this was hard for him, but I could also tell that he wanted to talk about it. He had a faraway look in his eye, as if trying to grab that memory and grapple with it.

"Dad told her to stay in Helena, but she told him, 'No,' she wanted to come home."

"Got any coffee?" he asked, followed by, "Want me to build a fire?"

I thought it would give him a break from the pain, and said, "That would be great."

I heard him chopping wood outside, while I started the coffee. Stomping feet on the porch announced his return. The door opened and he brought in an armful of wood and put it on the hearth. By the time, the aromatic smell of fresh brewed coffee filled the room, Luka had a fire blazing in the river rock fireplace.

We sat together on the couch to drink coffee, and he kissed me gently and sweetly on the mouth and resumed his story.

"She was just outside of Clancy, when a Greyhound bus, coming from Butte, hit ice and swerved into oncoming

248

traffic. Her car was hit head on, crushing it, before sending it hurtling over a 500-foot mountain cliff."

He stopped his story again. I waited, wondering how often he talked about her. He got up and stirred the fire with a poker. When he held up his empty coffee cup, I brought the pot into the living room and filled both of our cups.

"It took a week. A whole week, for the Sheriff's Department to recover her body."

There was another long pause. I could see it was hard for him to talk, and I gave him time, and only asked questions when I thought it would help.

"My Father, and I, of course, were devastated. I felt as if my guts had been ripped out. Her death was very physical for me. The physical pain was nearly unbearable. I couldn't understand why she hadn't taken me with her. She always took me with her. She took me everywhere," he said, his voice halting between tremors.

Not only had he lost his mother to terrible circumstances, but I felt instinctively he was suffering from survivor guilt. He stopped talking, his fist pressed against his mouth.

"Do you think my stepmother is beautiful?"

Surprised at the question I said, "Oh, yes. She is incredibly beautiful."

"My Mother was even more beautiful," he said.

"What?" I asked, a bit confused.

"Isabell is my Mother's younger sister."

"Wow, how do you feel about that?"

"I feel fine about it. I was 10 when my Mother died so suddenly, and so tragically. Isabell stepped in, helped raise me, took care of the house. She has the same common sense as my Mother," he looked at me and dispensed a small smile.

"She was perfect for my Dad. Remember, he was still a young man when my Mother was killed. There was no woman better for him than Isabell, besides my Mother, of course. She's a wonderful person. I can't say enough good things about her. My Father was incredibly fortunate to have had two great loves in his life."

"That's hard to imagine," I said.

"What? That my aunt is my stepmother."

"Yes, I guess so. Then Kyle and Josie must be your half-brother and half-sister?" I surmised.

"Yes," Luka said quietly.

"They are the best."

I reached out and touched his shoulder. He looked at me and said, "As inconceivable as it may be, out of great loss has come great happiness."

Luka's mood was somber when he kissed me good night. I thought he needed some private time. Talking about loss can be cathartic, but it can also be painful.

I sat bolt upright in bed as fear shot through me. What was that noise? My ears straining and sifting the sounds of the night. Ten seconds, twenty seconds, a half minute passed, as I struggled to identify the disturbance that woke me up.

In the dark, I pulled on a pair of pants, from the back of the bedside chair, topped my T-shirt with a hoodie, and over that my ancient parka.

I slipped the R9 handgun into the pocket of my jacket. I held my breath hoping to hear the sound repeated, but several more minutes passed, and there was only silence.

Suddenly, the sound came again. It was outside, whatever it was. I stepped to the window, moving the bedroom blind just enough to look out. I hugged the wall, motionless, breathless, waiting.

The moon light cast eerie shadows intensifying the anxiety and apprehension. I lingered in the shadows, expecting the sound to repeat. There was an urgency to pinpoint the source of my fear.

251

My patient surveillance finally paid off, when I caught sight of moving shadows in the driveway and the soft crunch of feet on gravel. The sound seemed to be slowly cautiously moving away from the cabin.

I was paralyzed by panic. I knew I might be forced to act. I waited, feeling that precipitous action might be worse than no action. Confused I held my position. I wondered if the nighttime visitors had been here before. As the two figures moved out of the shadows, I realized it was a pair of deer.

I felt myself folding. Everything was crashing down on me. The tragedy in Lake Oswego. The many months as a fugitive from justice. The never-ending anxiety and stress caused by pulse pounding fear. Every prayer, every precaution, useless against the whims of fate.

If it had been the FBI, they would have taken a battering ram to the door and I would be laying on the floor dead or in handcuffs.

I invoked my mantra, "Be cool. Look cool."

I'd had this feeling before. I knew it was my subconscious telling me it was about time to move on. I decided I could be gone by late tomorrow or early the following morning at the latest. I didn't want to wait any longer, but I knew I couldn't leave any sooner. I wanted to avoid any face-to-face goodbyes. It didn't give me much time, but I didn't want to run for Canada minus my clothes and all my money.

Luka. What about Luka? Should I write him a letter? Why? So, he'd have a souvenir? I didn't think a Dear Luka letter was appropriate. I needed to find a way to thank him, but time was a challenge to that effort.

I packed the Sportage with things I could live without, while keeping necessities in the cabin. Once I had the car loaded, I spent the early morning hours devising a new life plan. I watched the sun break the horizon before going outside.

I grabbed a shovel from the shed along with an old coffee can and walked to the creek and found a spot about twenty feet up the bank between a set of rocks and dug a hole.

Chapter Twenty Two

Outed

There was a winding path, just beyond the cabin door, that twisted playfully through an ancient stand of pines, where a shadowed creek sang its primitive song, and lichen clung to age old rocks. There was a meadow of golden grasses and the heady fragrance of moss and wildflowers enticed butterflies and bees, all dancing before a chain of blue mountains in the distance.

The winter had passed quickly, and life at the '*Grizzly Ranch*' was wonderfully simple. I'd been in hiding in this blessed wilderness since Luka and his family had discovered me sick and dehydrated at a rest area three months previously.

Like a lost puppy, they had brought me home and made me part of their family. They called me Lori, unaware of the ghosts of my past. Both literal and metaphorical. I had most everything packed and stowed in the Sportage. Destination undetermined.

I could already feel it. Regret like a pain in my chest. I loved it here, but I had no choice. It was a known law of the universe that nothing lasts forever. I had to leave. Survival the only goal.

I jumped, my feet physically leaving the hardwood floor. The rap on the door sounded like a thunderclap in my head. It was a weekday, and Luka was in Helena. I wasn't expecting any visitors. I turned from my sink of dirty dishes, apprehension pounding in my chest, wiped my wet hands, and hurried to answer it.

Luka dressed in worn jeans and a white Irish fisherman's sweater stood on the front porch. His face was dark with rage. I stepped back, allowing him to enter.

"No kiss?" I asked, humor my first defense mechanism.

My stomach churned with fear. I felt a new and heightened fear. A fear that my biggest supporter had turned on me. My mind raced to figure out what could have happened.

"Would you like a tea or coffee?" I asked, finding myself retreating to the standard protocols of civility.

"Stop the bullshit!" Luka bellowed.

I had never heard him raise his voice before, and I felt my legs turn to rubber and my mouth to the dryness of wood pulp.

I grabbed the corner of the kitchen island to steady myself and looked out the window to the forest of pines and

255

the clouds hanging like cotton balls in a flawless early spring sky.

"Sit your ass down, we need to clear up a few things."

I took several deep breaths and pushed off from the island like a swimmer from the block and sat in a chair across from the fuming giant with the angry amber eyes.

"As I'm sure you know, Kyle has a crush on you. He's a little embarrassed because his big brother seems to be in the game, he'd like to be playing in."

I felt my eyelids close. My tightly clenched fist found my mouth as if to stifle a scream.

"He wanted to check out your high school picture. So, he went online and found out that you did not attend Annie Wright's. Curious, he checked and found out you didn't attend nursing school at OHSU," his voice as sharp as a razor.

My eyelids seemed glued shut. I had no more lies to tell and I didn't want to see his anger or the hurt in his eyes.

"Fucking look at me," he hissed his rage barely corralled.

"Okay," I said prying my eyes open, "I'll get my things packed and be out of here no later than tomorrow. I promise, you'll never even know I was here."

"No, fucking way. I want to know who the hell you are and what mischief you are up to."

I was on the event horizon spiraling helplessly toward a black hole and total disintegration. There was no answer I could give, that would fix the damage my lies had done.

I wanted to cry but crying would not help and would probably only make things worse. This was not a time for frailty or weakness.

"I want to thank you and your family for your kindness. You, especially. You have been extraordinary."

"Well thanks, I'm really impressed with your humility and gratitude," he said irritably. "Stop dancing around my questions."

"Who, the fuck, are you? I want to know your name."

"I can imagine how disappointed you must be in me."

"Disappointed isn't the right word. Seething rage would be a closer description."

Luka threw his words like hand grenades at me.

"I want you to can the crap and tell me who you are and what's going on. My family and I trusted you, we made you part of our family."

"Luka, please just hold me. My life is in shambles. Every day of my life is mind spinning madness. I'm terrified," I said with more honesty than I had mustered in many months.

I sat, staring at the ground, just waiting for the last thread of my life to snap.

"Come over here," he said, motioning to a spot on the couch next to him.

When he put his arm around me, I felt those unwanted tears begin to slide down my cheeks.

"Okay, let's start with who you are?"

"My name is," I could hardly form the words, "Sky Evenson."

"Sky Evenson?" He repeated my name trying to tie a headline to it.

"The high school kid that's killed four people. That's who you are?" he said standing abruptly with unvarnished shock, his eyes literally rolling toward the ceiling.

"I haven't killed anybody. I swear to you. I've been on the run trying to keep from being killed."

"I'm listening," he said looking down at me.

"I don't even know where to start."

"The beginning would be a good place," Luka encouraged.

"It's going to take a while."

"I don't have a date, so anytime you want to get started is good.

I laughed out loud through a haze of tears. I was pleased to see his expression soften as I started recounting the whole rotten saga.

"I grew up in Lake Oswego, Oregon. My Dad is NBA basketball star forward, Cal Evenson," Just saying my Dad is 'Cal Evenson' usually draws a comment of some sort, but apparently Luka already knew that tidbit of Sky Evenson's history.

"My Mother is Cassie Cornell Evenson, the jewelry designer. We live next door to U.S. Speaker of the House, Jerry Johnson. Johnson's stepson, Cory Davis, was one of my best friends."

"Someone killed Cory, in Indiana a couple months ago. My other friend Ward Haskins was killed at the same time. They were buried together in a single shallow grave on a vacant property outside of Indianapolis. Apparently, they were tortured and mutilated before they were killed execution style."

"Is there any chance you could get me a Coke?" I asked Luka, "I'm really thirsty."

"Sure, if you promise you aren't going to try to make a run for it."

"I don't have the strength to walk across the room," I confessed.

He brought me the chilled soda from the kitchen and a glass of ice.

I took a swallow of cola from the bottle before filling the glass.

"Cory loathed his stepfather with an intensity that is hard to convey. Truly his hatred bordered on mental illness. It was pathological. I sometimes wondered if Johnson had sexually abused Cory when he was little. I mean Cory's hatred was boundless. He spent half of his waking hours trying to find dirt on Johnson. He was determined that his mother leave the Speaker."

I paused and took a couple more swallows of the Coke trying to wet my mouth enough to keep talking.

"The news reports say that you and your friends stole Top Secret materials and were in the process of passing them onto a Chinese spy network. You in fact, are said to have been actively working on Facebook to arouse Antifa supporters."

"Only partly true. Cory stole compromising information on Johnson unrelated to United States secrets."

"That sounds intriguing," he said.

"The rest is a pack of lies spun by Jerry Johnson to protect himself," I gave him a sour look and said, "I need to tell you how this happened without interruption, okay?"

"Okay, sorry."

"So, Ward, and I were over at the Johnson house on a Saturday night hanging out with Cory and my main squeeze, Cory's brother Chad. It was early June of last year. The Speaker and Mrs. Johnson were out of town doing fund raising for his 2022 campaign. Cory was doing what he was always doing, trying to break into the Speaker's computer."

I paused gathering my thoughts.

"Cory had been playing with computers since he was a toddler and was a computer genius in every sense," I paused and looked in Luka's direction. He said nothing, and I continued, "So that night, Cory got past all the firewall protections. We told him to shut it down, but he was too far down the rabbit-hole. He said he knew he was about to find something big, something that would finally make his mother see Johnson for the psychopath that he was."

"Are you getting hungry?"

"I don't feel like cooking anything," I said wearily, "but, if you are hungry, maybe I can find you something."

"I was thinking I could put something together for us. Why don't you sit here and calm down while I check out what's in the fridge?"

Truthfully, I was glad for the break. I was quaking like a leaf in a fall storm, as those memories came back with a vengeance.

"What about a couple banana splits? You've got a ton of ice cream, there's bananas here, and every topping imaginable," he announced somewhat gleefully.

"No, thanks. I don't want anything sweet right now."

"Hey, there's a pot of leftover spaghetti here from the other night. I could warm it up for us."

"Leftovers. Great. There's parmesan cheese on the door of the frig and there's fresh French bread in the bread box," I hollered back.

After filling up on the leftover spaghetti we resumed our positions. It took me a couple minutes to organize my thoughts before I continued.

"We all told Cory he was going to get us killed but there was no stopping him. He was obsessed."

"Obsession can be a dangerous thing," Luka volunteered.

"Ward was playing some game on his phone while Chad and I played chess. When Cory reappeared, he was as pale as a ghost. I mean he looked as if he had just seen the ghost of his dead Father. We asked half a dozen times what was going on before he finally said, 'you guys need to come look at this crap.'"

"I wasn't obsessed with finding shit on the Speaker, so I wasn't particularly interested in pawing around in the Speaker's private business. I was afraid we could end up in prison for hacking a government official's computer. Aaron Swartz ended up dead and all he tried to do was pirate a few hundred thousand academic papers."

"But Cory insisted. Because we had never seen Cory so upset, we all headed into the Speaker's home office and pulled up chairs in front of the computer."

"The first thing that Cory displayed on the screen were pictures of the Speaker with convicted sex trafficker Jeffrey Epstein and his suspected procuress, Ghislaine Maxwell. There were at least half a dozen pictures that were obviously taken at different times and each of them appeared to be at parties or events."

"We looked from one to another assuming that was the bombshell Cory wanted us to see. I didn't like the vibe and started to stand up and Cory told me to sit back down."

I stopped and looked at Luka, trying to judge his mood. He was stone-faced.

"Remember, sugar, I'm an attorney. I've heard a lot of shit. Please, continue."

"I was a fucking virgin. And as far as I knew so were Cory, Chad, and Ward. We were all as innocent as angels. I'd only had a couple dozen dates in my entire sexless life. The pictures that Cory began scrolling through showed images of Jerry Johnson naked in every sexually explicit position you can imagine. I mean some were really disturbing. Can you imagine someone peeing on your face?"

He nodded. Apparently, he could imagine such things.

"The most alarming part about the pictures were the girls. Some of them looked twelve or thirteen at the most. I mean some of them barely had breast buds. Some appeared to be crying. There were hundreds of images. We were looking at the most depraved and disgusting pictures imaginable. Totally illegal child porn."

I stifled a sob and slowly shook my head, as though trying to clear it like an etch-a-sketch.

"Cory kept us prisoners to the computer. We spent over an hour and a half looking at still photos and videos. Incredible, revolting, repulsive videos. I was in shock. I-I think I have PTSD from the shock of it."

"A politician being a dangerous sexual predator, that doesn't surprise me," Luka said his mouth a rigid line.

"Oh, he's a hell of a lot worse than that," I said angrily.

"Cory made four copies on flash-drives. One for each of us." I didn't want the damn thing, but he said, that there was probably going to be fireworks, dangerous fireworks and he wanted to make sure we each had some insurance to protect ourselves just in case things went sideways. 'Sideways' seems like such a mundane word for the disaster that resulted."

I put my head in my hands, and said, "Luka I'm exhausted. Is there any chance we can finish this tomorrow?"

He checked the time on his phone.

"It's still early. Quite honestly, I am afraid that you will take off. Your record of flight to avoid prosecution is well known."

"I'm not going to run."

"Lori, I mean Sky, your record on truth telling is abysmal. I noticed that you have your car packed."

265

"Right you are," I said, caught in another lie.

Everything he knew about me had been a lie. My life had been twisted and distorted until sometimes I had trouble keeping reality and fantasy straight. I leaned back against the couch for support and trudged on with the story of my descent from normalcy to frantic fugitive.

"The Speaker and Mrs. Johnson came home a couple days later. At first there seemed to be no fireworks, or repercussions. The proverbial quiet before the storm. We were preparing for graduation, there was a lot of excitement around that."

"The summer was going to be a big deal for all of us. I was going back to France for my third summer of French emersion. Ward, who was a great sailor had signed up to work as a crewmember on a sailboat taking tourists around the San Juan Islands. Cory, although more subdued than usual, seemed excited to be going on a two-month long bike tour of Europe before heading off to USC."

"I tried to put the Jerry Johnson connection to Jeffrey Epstein out of my mind. I had wanted to talk to my parents about it, but the time had never been right. I couldn't forget the images of those young girls and worried about Johnson having access to more children. But I was also painfully aware that coming forward could lead to explosive repercussions and unimaginable problems."

266

I had to put my hand on my knee to keep it from thumping.

"Ward and I had talked about it one afternoon while we were waiting for Cory to pick us up to go to graduation practice. Ward said he wanted it to all just go away. He was angry that Cory had gotten us involved. He said he felt bad about the girls but felt that Jerry Johnson was too powerful for us to take on."

"I knew that the secrets of the Speaker's life could not stay hidden forever. However, I didn't think that I could be the one to spearhead his unmasking. I also didn't think Cory and Chad should expose their mother to the public humiliation. I wondered privately if perhaps that was why Cory had kept everything quiet."

I gave a brief tragic laugh. An involuntary reaction I hoped that Luka didn't misunderstand.

"It was the worst decision possible. Our inaction, our cowardness, our running away from the crime scene did nothing but make it worse," I said focusing my attention on the wood floor planks.

"For the first time since this whole thing began, I have begun to accept the totality of my responsibility. The crushing weight of that acceptance is an indescribable pain," I said sadly.

"It's all my fault. I couldn't expect Cory and Chad to do anything and Ward was his own person. If nothing else, I should have at least tried."

Luka took my hand and held it for a moment and then used it to pull me close and kissed me deeply. It was a kiss I wanted to drown in.

With the touch of his index finger, he raised my chin, leaving me to see nothing but his eyes. He swallowed me with his arms, pulling me tight against his body. His mouth against mine, his teeth nibbled and pulled at my lips, teasing and exciting me with his tongue. Arousing my buried sexual desires.

I ran my fingertips across his facial stubble, and Luka leaned into my touch and closed his eyes. I slipped my fingertips into his mouth and he sucked on each one tenderly. His tongue renewing its exploration of my mouth, pushed me back, slipping his hand under my shirt.

Luka stood up suddenly and found a playlist of slow dance numbers on YouTube. He looked at me for approval and I nodded. He sat the phone down on a side table and we danced to the long version of B.B. King's "The Thrill Is Gone" my head resting on his chest.

After the dance we stood in the middle of the kitchen just holding onto each other.

"I have to tell you I'm still confused about our relationship. Although I've felt a growing bond between us, I have had severe reservations. There has been something nagging at me, holding me back. Something has kept me uneasy."

I said nothing.

"I have never believed your story. I knew something wasn't right. I've never felt our relationship was ready for prime time. I didn't know why you were lying but I knew you were no more 23 than I'm Bradley Cooper. In fact, I have worried that you might not even be eighteen.

At least that explained why he wouldn't consummate our relationship I thought.

"I guess what you are telling me tonight confirms my suspicions.

"I am so sorry. I have spent the last nearly nine months on the run. I never wanted to lie to you. Everything I have done has been for self-preservation. I've just been trying to stay alive."

He kissed me on the forehead and then the top of the head like a small child. It reminded me of how Mateo would sometimes respond to me when I was at my most vulnerable.

"I'm having trouble focusing on anything but your breasts."

"Do you want me to tell you what happened? We can wait if you want?"

"Honey," he said as he touched the front of my shirt, "I need to hear the rest of this horror story, tonight."

"Okay," I said stupidly, trying once again to find the thread of the tale.

I knew he was trying to make the telling of my story easier, more relaxed, but the interruptions had sent me off track again. He put his hands on my neck and shoulders and gently kneaded my tightened muscles.

"It was two in the morning the day after graduation when Cory called me. He was sobbing and sounded close to hysteria. I had never heard him in such a state. He said that he and Ward were hiding in my boathouse."

"Boathouse?"

"We live on the Lake," I said, "Lake Oswego."

"Got it."

"I snuck out the kitchen slider to the back patio. I opened the boathouse land door and softly called their names. It took a minute or two before the guys climbed out of the boat. Cory was in bad shape. He was soaking wet. He had a black eye and a cut lip, and his T shirt was ripped. I gave him

270

a towel and a pair of my brother's sweats from a storage cabinet."

"Ward seemed to be unhurt, but he was clearly upset. He was talking rapidly, the words coming so fast I had to tell him a couple times to slow down. Eventually he told me that Cory had given his mother a copy of the file that morning and she had gone on a rampage. She smashed glassware, shredded the Speaker's clothes, and seemed to have lost her mind. She pulled out an underwear drawer and retrieved a .22 pistol and she told Cory she was going to kill Jerry when he got home."

"An understandable reaction," Luka chimed in.

"Fuckin' a. Anyway, Cory told Ward he didn't believe her but decided to stay home and make sure that she didn't kill the Speaker. He wanted the Speaker in jail, not his mother. Ward said he came over to keep Cory company while he waited for Johnson to come home from a meeting."

"I stood looking at them, trying to locate my brain. I needed to hear the rest of the story. Cory was close to catatonic. He was in shock and was unable to talk. I didn't want to pressure Cory, so I looked to Ward to tell me what happened."

"According to Ward, he and Cory had smoked a couple of joints and had fallen asleep in the basement family room. They hadn't heard Johnson come home but were awakened to the sounds of screaming and muffled gun shots."

271

"Oh, no," Luka said, playing the role of Greek chorus.

"I hadn't heard anything that sounded like a disturbance and certainly had not heard any gunfire. Like I said I lived right next door. But next door isn't like in most neighborhoods. The houses are quite a distance apart. There's a lot of landscape buffer, to enhance privacy. The lake is our backyard. I lived on one side of the Johnson's and Ward lived on the other side of the Johnsons."

"Okay, that helps me visualize the setting."

"Cory gave Ward his car keys and asked him to move his car over on to Lake Shore Terrace. Cory said he wouldn't go upstairs until he knew his car had been moved and that Ward was safe in the Evenson boathouse. He said he didn't know if his mother had killed Jerry or Jerry had killed his Mother. And what about Chad? He seemed to be MIA, but the silence that had taken over the house had them terrified."

"I took Cory in my arms and just held him, rocking gently, knowing that something terrible had happened."

Luka took my hand and said, "Take a couple of breaths. I can imagine this was quite a traumatic series of events."

I was reliving the agony of that night all over again and had begun to hyperventilate. Luka brought me another Coke and a couple Tylenol.

He wrapped his arm around me and said, "Just wait until you're ready."

It took several minutes but I finally got control of my breathing and could continue the story.

"Cory and I held our embrace for several minutes until he finally pulled away and collapsed into a nearby lounge chair. His lip was quivering when he finally found his voice.

"That son-of-a-bitch killed Mom and Chad."

"I couldn't speak, I became physically ill. Cindy Johnson was my Mother's best friend. She was like an aunt to me. I-I loved her."

"Cory's brother Chad was a year older than us. He had been my first crush. My first date. He had in fact, given me my first kiss. We were still sort of seeing each other when he was home from college. I was devastated. Heartbroken to tell you the truth."

"Cory blamed himself. He was grief stricken. He was sick with the pain of guilt."

"That's how it was when my mother died. It was as if someone had ripped out my guts.

Cory had finally decided to break his silence and had told his mother that the four of us had uncovered the Speaker's dirty secret and had copies to prove it."

"Apparently when Cindy confronted Jerry, she told him about the four of us discovering his sexual deviance and that there were flash drives."

Luka nodded his head.

"Cory stammered and told us he went upstairs after Ward left and found his mother lying in a pool of dark coagulated blood on the floor of the kitchen. His brother he told us was lying face down framed in blood on the floor of the dining room."

"Cory described being overwhelmed with grief, he described falling on his mother's body and sobbing. He said suddenly Johnson and his lead security man walked into the room and when Cory saw Johnson, he lost his mind and attacked him. Andy the security guy used his mace and a club to defend Johnson. Cory took out the back door with Andy hot on his heels. Cory said he jumped in the lake and left Andy standing flatfooted in the yard. He then swam to our boathouse where he was supposed to meet Ward."

"Shit!" Luka exclaimed, showing his first flash of emotion.

"Desperate times," I hesitated, took a breath and then a swallow of Coke.

"We knew we were in trouble. We knew Jerry was going to manipulate the story. We had no idea however, that within 24 hours, the three of us would be characterized as

Master criminals behind two murders, computer hacking, theft, espionage, assault with the intent to kill, and flight to avoid prosecution."

"We kept wondering why there were no sirens or cops on the scene yet, but then we figured it only made sense since Jerry was probably making some crime scene adjustments. I suspected that Jerry wanted to have the FBI on the scene first due to his political position."

"We decided to make a run for it. We would each head in a different direction. Ward was headed to Canada. Cory to New York. I said I was just going to keep moving, going from town to town, destination undetermined. That was the last time I ever saw them. They left the boathouse and walked down my driveway and disappeared into the darkness."

"I snuck back into my house. In my bathroom I pulled my hair into a tight ponytail and then with a pair of scissors cut my hair right to the rubber band. I saved the ponytail, putting it in a plastic bag. I didn't want anyone to know I had cut my hair, so I stuck the severed ponytail in a backpack along with a few clothes and toiletries."

"I walked out of the house, got in my car and drove away. I walked into a Seattle, Washington Wells Fargo branch at 9:00 a.m. the following morning and emptied my bank account."

"The $7,500 in the account was the money I had saved for my summer trip to France. Once the money was in my purse, I surrendered my debit card to the teller who shredded it."

"I parked my car in a mall parking lot outside Tacoma, Washington. I wrote down all the phone numbers from my cell phone contact list. I then cleared it of all entries and tossed the phone on the floor of the car. I locked the vehicle, put the key in an envelope along with a note telling my Mom where it was parked and dropped the envelope into the corner mailbox. I called Uber and was soon at Sea-Tac airport buying a ticket to Denver."

"In Denver I rented a hotel room and bleached my hair and added green and aqua highlights. A stop at Target gave me the right clothes to match my hair and makeup. I went to a dollar store and bought a pair of horn-rimmed eyeglasses."

"After a night in Denver I went to the Amtrak station and bought a ticket to Dallas, Texas."

"By the time I got to Dallas I had managed to completely change my looks, going from Preppie to Punk. I found a motel in Dallas and stayed there until I bought my Sportage through a Craigslist ad."

"Once I had wheels I just kept moving, with a few stops in between. Within a couple months on the road, I had lost thirty-five pounds and had become Lori Cameron."

Chapter Twenty Three

Keep Talking

"What about the Kawasaki sport bike?"

"What?" totally confused by the question, which seemed to have no relationship to what had happened last year in Lake Oswego.

"I checked with the Illinois Department of Motor Vehicles and that bike was reported stolen in early January, just before we picked you up at the Rest Area."

"Do we need to talk about the bike now?"

"Damn right we do!" his anger flaming up once again.

"It's not something I'm proud of."

"I imagine not."

"Not for the reasons you are assuming," I answered with my own undisguised anger.

"I'm waiting," he said with noticeable irritation.

I put the palm of my hand over my face. I didn't even know where to start.

"Fuck," I felt my teeth grinding and the hand that had been covering my face raked through my hair.

"I was living in Middletown, Illinois. I had started selling my jewelry line to shops in Chicago. One day I took the train to the city to deliver an order to a shop on the Magnificent Mile."

"The shop was selling a lot of my stuff. That afternoon the owner had arranged without my knowledge to introduce me to a man named Hayes Benton. Hayes said his Mother was interested in featuring my jewelry line at two shops she owned in Manhattan."

"I don't want to talk about this," I said my eyes finally settling on his.

"At this point I don't think you have much choice."

I stood up and paced, shame and embarrassment acting as the fuel. I wondered if I could control the temper tantrum that was lurking just below the surface. I walked toward the kitchen, putting space between us.

"Hayes is a very handsome man comfortable in $5,500 suits, $1,000 silk shirts, and $400 an ounce cologne. Like any sociopath he is exceedingly charming. He took me to lunch, and before I knew it, I agreed to go up to Winnetka to a house he was staying at on Lake Michigan."

I paused, focusing on the fire.

279

"We spent the afternoon snowmobiling, ate a fabulous dinner, watched a movie, and then had sex."

Sensing my humiliation, he said easily, "You are not the only person that ever had a one-night stand."

I laughed and said stupidly, "Is it common for a person who has had only one sexual experience in her entire 'effin life to suddenly jump to one-night stands?"

"Time and circumstance," was his only comment.

"After I got out of the shower, I heard Hayes in the bedroom talking on his cell phone. I was sure he was talking about me. He told the person on the phone to cool it that he had everything under control. He just needed a bit of time to do what needed to be done."

"I believed the person on the phone with him was Jerry Johnson. I was terrified I didn't know what to do, I just kept playing the friendly sex partner game that he was playing. I was his prisoner for 19 days."

"He held you prisoner?"

He made every moment with me seem completely natural. He loves sports. He liked to play all day and screw all night."

"But there was another vibe. The doors were always locked. I was never out of his sight. I felt he was holding me prisoner. It was a gentle kind of imprisonment, but it was imprisonment. By day two I knew I would have to be patient and wait for the right time to make my move. I figured I would get only one chance to escape. It took nineteen days before I had that opportunity."

"I waited until I was sure he was asleep before I slipped out of the house using his lifted key card. I got into the garage, found the Kawasaki Ninja and was about to leave when Hayes came into the garage. He tried to charm me out of my fear and my intention to leave. I'd only been out of the bed less than five minutes, but he had noticed and was going to fix that mistake fast. He was as smooth and persuasive as he had been for the last nearly three weeks."

"He tried to charm me out of my fear and my intention to leave. I'm convinced he had no idea I had heard the phone call. But by then I was doubting the meaning of the phone call and worried that I was wrong about any affiliation Hayes had to Jerry Johnson."

"He was easing himself closer and closer to me, talking to me as if I was a panicked child. When he was close enough, I hit him as hard as I could with a fish bat and followed with a powerful kick to his head."

"I bet that pissed him off," Luka smirked.

"I knocked him senseless, but he didn't lose consciousness. In fact, he managed to partially block my escape."

"Are you sure this guy is working for Johnson?"

"No. Sometimes I think I was having a psychotic break."

"After he was on his knees, I opened the garage door and headed back to Chicago on the Kawasaki. About fifteen minutes later he and the chauffer caught up with me. I took the bike up a trail off the highway. They followed me off the road with the Snow Runner."

"Hayes kept calling to me, telling me to "cut the crap and come back." I stayed on the trail and prayed for the best. They were in that big ass Snow Runner and had no way of keeping up with me on the sport bike. The chauffer took several shots at me. I think they were trying to scare me into stopping."

"I was afraid to leave the bike, so I took it with me. So, I did steal it, but not like a thief would steal something."

"Okay, not like a thief would steal something. Got it," he said, with a look of feeble acceptance.

"So where does your friend Mateo fit into all this?"

282

I had hoped to skirt Mateo's involvement in this nightmare, but it didn't sound like Luka was going to let that happen.

"What does Mateo have to do with this?"

"That's what I want to find out?"

"I'd tell you to get the hell out of here, but it's your house."

"No, it's my father's house."

I went to the slider and stepped outside onto the balcony.

I was barely able to keep from attacking him with my fists and feet. I had so much anger and fear bottled up inside that I was like a volcano ready to erupt. I took gulps of cool air and tried to get control of my anger. Luka stood in the doorway looking at me.

"Mateo has nothing to do with any of this," I said firmly.

"I think he does," Luka answered.

"Fuck you," I said irritably.

"Whoa girl. Apparently, I've hit a nerve. It seems this man means a great deal to you. I don't want to harm him. I just need to know where he fits into the story."

My eyes burned into him.

"Come here."

"It's late. I'm exhausted. I feel as if I'm coming apart at the seams."

"Well come over here so I can check those seams. You look like you're about to hit me. I just want to warn you, kickboxer or not, I can take you out."

"What?" I said, quietly shaking my head.

Mentally I was trying to tape myself back together, but I didn't know if that was even possible. I felt as if I had been dismembered a tiny piece at a time. It was as if I had left chunks of myself at every stop, I'd made over the last nearly ten months. In fact, there now seemed to be a huge missing piece right at the middle of my core. I walked into his outstretched arms.

"I'm barely holding it together," I mumbled.

"You've had a bad run recently. I can't even imagine what you have gone through."

I felt my forehead pucker as I looked into his eyes. I knew our relationship had no future. I had a $300,000 reward on my head and was facing 4 murder charges and a list of felonies 2 pages long. I could not cut him loose, nor could I commit. I knew he was just trying to protect his heart, to be prepared for whatever was coming.

"Are you going to run back to Mateo if we get this mess all straightened out? You said you had thought you loved him. Do you want to be with him?"

I looked at my feet and said, "I don't know, Luka. I-I-I don't know."

He releases his embrace and sighs, "That's fair."

His eyes captured mine.

"I want to help. And I promise, I can, and I will help. To start with you are going to need a damn good lawyer. I am volunteering my firm for that job. I will oversee the case, but I will not be your attorney of record. Secondly, you're going to need big money. I'm worried you will be denied bond no matter how much money we wave at them. We're looking at four potential murder charges in two different states. It's going to be tricky. I can see where the court will demand you put up at least $10,000,000 or be able to secure a bond for that amount. We are going to need a sympathetic judge that's for sure. Otherwise, your sweet ass will be in jail until the trial."

"Oh, Sweet Zeus," I moaned, "$10,000,000. My parents don't have that kind of cash floating around."

"I think I can work something on that score," he said.

I said nothing. My brain was an empty shell.

He continued, probing my eyes, "I just want to make sure when we come out on the other side of this nightmare, I'm not going to have expectations that make it difficult for either one of us."

I didn't know what else I could say. My emotions were a tangled knot, and I didn't know who would be able to untangle the mess.

"I need to sit down again or I'm going to fall down. These late nights are killing me. What time is it anyway?"

He pulled his handheld from his pocket and tapped the screen, "1:20. Let's go back inside. I'll make us some tea. Isabell says a cup of warm tea sooths the soul."

I sat down at the kitchen island and allowed Luka to make me a cup of tea.

"I met Mateo while I was in Mexico working with Aunt Janet the summer before my senior year. Janet is a Nurse Practitioner. She was working with the Mexican poor. I was her Nursing Assistant. We did wellness checks, gave vaccinations, patched up cuts, set broken bones, delivered babies. You name it we did it."

"Thanks for the tea. Is there any ice cream?" I found myself nearly sniveling.

"Keep talking while I round up something for us."

"There's really little to tell. Mateo was born in Seattle, Washington. His Mom is a teacher at University of Washington. His Dad is a Mexican national who is a delegate to the Mexican Embassy in Seattle.

After Mateo graduated from Fordham University, he had a great offer to go to work for the Mexican government and so he went to Mexico. Since then, he has challenged the New York bar and is licensed to practice law in New York. He is trying to keep his options open."

"He speaks flawless English and Spanish. We met and just hit it off. He was very respectful. He knew I was a virgin. He was incredibly kind to me. We spent a lot of time together that summer and he sent me home a virgin despite my best efforts to end that situation."

I saw Luka smile and then he said, "Okay, but there's more to it than that."

"After the killings in Lake Oswego I traveled to Texas. I crossed the border, into Mexico. My plan was to hide out in Belize. But the manhunt and its growing reward made me rethink the craziness of that idea. I was terrified of being grabbed by Mexican bounty hunters or locked up in a Mexican prison."

"I didn't want to put Mateo at risk, but I figured if anybody could get me back into the U.S. it would be him.

287

He's a Captain in the Jalisco State Police. I put his job, his future, everything he is working for in jeopardy."

"I reached out to him. He let me stay at his home outside of Guadalajara for two weeks during the height of the manhunt. This was just after the bodies of Cory and Ward had been discovered in Indiana. The media and law enforcement were banging the drum for my capture. During that time, we became sexually intimate. He risked everything to help me. He believes I'm innocent. He gave me money. I can't allow him to be implicated in this nightmare."

"So, Mateo knows the whole story?"

"No, just what he's seen on television. I was in bad shape physically and psychologically when I got to his place. I could barely talk. I felt I was in the middle of a nervous breakdown on a downward trajectory. Mateo supported me in every way imaginable. I will never forget his kindness."

"I felt he might need some insurance, so I hid a copy of the Jerry Johnson thumb drive at his house. I didn't tell him about that until he was getting on a plane from Laredo back to Guadalajara. That's the whole story, until I fell into your arms at the Rest Area."

"A cop and a lawyer, huh? He has put himself at incredible risk on your behalf. He could be facing criminal charges and a stint in a Mexican jail himself if his participation in assisting you ever comes out. We will need to

288

proceed with great caution. I don't want anyone going to jail but Johnson and his co-conspirators."

"Promise?"

"Of course. I think Mateo must care very deeply for you."

A weak smile was my only response.

"The last question I have is where did you get the guns?"

"I had an agreement with the owner of the Middletown house. I cleaned up the property in exchange for anything I wanted to keep or sell. I wanted to keep the guns. I have the paperwork. Obviously, I couldn't register them."

"To the best of your knowledge have those weapons been used in any criminal activities?"

"No. I kept them for self-defense."

"Are you going to turn me in?" I asked.

I knew he heard me, but he gave no immediate answer.

"I guess there is one more thing I need to tell you."

"What's that?" his face thoughtful.

"I made another copy of the Johnson flash drive and buried it out by the creek."

"Our creek?"

"Yes, between two rocks about 150 yards down the trail."

"Wow. Things may have just gotten a whole lot easier. We'll have to recover that tomorrow," Luka said.

"Please. I need to know. Are you calling the FBI?"

"We need a plan first," he said giving me a reassuring smile, "But, yes, we need to contact the FBI and arrange for you to turn yourself in."

Chapter Twenty Four

Home Bound

"I'm going to go camp out at the main house. No matter how badly I want to stay here tonight, I don't think it's a good idea. I want you to know I've had the gate sensor disconnected. You can't get out the gate without a code. You having your rig packed makes me uncomfortable. I don't want to take your keys, in case of some weird emergency and you need to get to the main house fast. But I can't let you leave. Dial 99 from the land line if you want anything or call me on my cell. Okay?"

Well, that was a surprise. I was now basically under house arrest.

I knew Luka was right to leave. He needed to clear his head and digest everything I had told him. And I needed time to reassemble my dismantled mind.

Just talking about Mateo had brought back sweet memories that had been submerged just below the surface. I missed him, and the wall I built around his memory was crumbling.

And Hayes, that Mother Fucker, I missed him too. I was beginning to think Hayes had become my sexual obsession. I wanted him and I felt guilty for those passionate emotions. At least I can report I'm not pregnant.

I was more confused about Luka than ever before. I was exhausted and I knew I wasn't thinking straight. I felt as if I had been 'dragged across concrete,' remembering the movie I had watched with Hayes.

My plan to sneak out before dawn was now sidetracked. Luka said he would start working on a legal plan for me, but I was not confident that staying put was the answer.

I went to bed fully clothed, with gun and burn phone within reach. I dozed off quickly. I opened my eyes groggy and disoriented. A herd of elephants was stampeding through my head.

There were muffled footsteps on the front porch. My heart was racing. I hopped from the bed and stood motionless, trying to control my breathing, waiting for another sound of movement. I needed to know if the deer were back, or it was something more sinister. I needed to know if I needed to run.

"Be cool. Look cool," I said, over and over under my breath.

I felt a hitch in my breathing as I strained to hear the sound repeated. Was it an intruder? I heard nothing. I needed to know was it a real threat or just an imagined one.

292

There was no answer at Luka's number. I dialed 99 from the land phone, left it off the hook and let it ring. I quietly opened the sliding door and squinted into the darkness. I didn't know what was waiting out there, but I knew I couldn't hesitate.

I moved on to the balcony. I swung over the railing and slid down a support post onto the lower patio. I let go of the post and turned around. Instinctively I assumed an orthodox fight stance. Ready to take down the shadow blocking my escape. I kept my hands up to protect my chin and I bobbed and weaved to stay out of his grasp.

"Come on bitch, let me see whatcha' got," his gravelly voice taunted.

He lunged towards me. He was big and clumsy, and I was able to quickly convert that to my advantage. I let him pass by on my left and then broke his knee. He went down on one knee and I followed up with a series of quick kicks to his face.

In one final mind-numbing round house kick I sent him toppling over. Once he was down, I centered myself over the top of him and drove fist after fist into his face. My coach had trained me to maintain my attack until the opponent could no longer respond.

I decided to pull his body behind the wood pile, hiding it from view. My eyes scanned the yard, seeing nothing

I raced into the trees. I was running again. I hadn't been choosing my own course for a long time now. And once again, I was a puppet reacting only to the directions of my puppet master.

Thirty feet into the trees I stopped and crouched in a thicket of undergrowth and waited. I saw the lights flash on in my bedroom. I continued to watch, and then I saw a shadowed figure emerge from the bedroom onto the balcony talking into a handheld device. He paced the balcony scanning the yard and the forest beyond with a powerful spotlight for any signs of life. After a brief conversation he disconnected and went back into the house. I couldn't tell if it was Hayes, but I suspected it was.

The chill nipped my face. I was glad that I had put on my parka before leaving the cabin. I knew it was going to get cold before the night was over. I stayed in the heavy undergrowth, afraid to run in case my departure might be heard. The mystery man stayed in the cabin for nearly fifteen minutes.

I could see the fat guy that I'd hobbled had been able to stand up.

"Help, help. I'm hurt. I need help!" I heard the fat guy holler.

I had hoped he would have been out longer, but he was up and had begun to cause a disturbance. The man in the cabin emerged through the basement slider and jogged to the injured man.

"What the hell happened?"

"She fucking broke my knee, and probably a couple of ribs and damn sure my nose. I can hardly breathe."

"How long ago?"

"I don't know. She cold cocked me, almost as soon as I came outside."

"Fuck. Let's get you inside and cleaned up. I'm not done in there."

I watched as the tall slender man in the shadows helped the stupid one limp into the house. My mind raced. Most of my belongings were stowed in the Sportage I didn't think they had figured that out. I assumed he was going through my computer and some paperwork that I had left out on the desk.

Long white fingers of the car's spotlight reached into the forest undergrowth where they poked and prodded, seemingly examining every leaf and limb. The battered grey Jeep inched slowly up the gravel road, less than a quarter of a mile from the cabin. The sound of tires on the gravel would stop every few feet and the vehicle's engine would fall into idle while the driver manually directed the powerful beam of a large spotlight slowly into the blackness of the deep woods, patiently searching.

I took a single step back and pressed myself hard against a giant pine tree, barely able to breathe, my heart fluttering uselessly in my chest. I stood with a death grip on the R9 Stealth semiautomatic, waiting and watching, as the beam of light crept slowly from tree to thicket, less than three feet from where I hid.

I heard the engine's rhythm change, as the driver shifted the transmission into drive. I watched as the Jeep moved forward down the road. I felt my muscles relax. The process of stopping and spotlighting the woods was repeated several more times before I saw the driver turn the vehicle sharply around at a wide spot in the road and head back in my direction.

The driver appeared to be the fat one. Where was his friend? The Jeep accelerated suddenly, sending sprays of gravel from the vehicle's back tires, causing its battered body to slide from side to side before its tires caught traction, digging two deep bilateral tracks up the road leading back to the cabin.

In utter blackness, I allowed myself to exhale, and with that exhalation, came a series of body jerking shivers. My eyes burned from old tears. After several minutes of rigid stillness, I took a tentative step forward.

The canopy of trees obscured the moon. My eyes struggled to penetrate the blackness, as I moved cautiously toward the road. I took one hesitant step followed by another, moving tentatively toward the road, leaves and branches slapping my face. I continued to strain my eyes against the darkness, just trying to see the ground in front of me. There was a cracking sound and I felt myself tumbling forward.

As I fell, I rolled into a somersault attempting to limit the impact. I heard an agonized gasp escape through my tightly pinched lips, as my jaw slammed against the ground. The impact sent me sprawling onto the hard, damp ground and my clenched fists slid painfully across rocks and tree roots.

The musky smells of the forest bed filled my nostrils. I laid in the dirt and foliage dazed and disoriented for several minutes, my legs and arms outstretched awkwardly. My jaw ached, my knuckles were scraped, and my left ankle was twisted painfully. To my relief, I felt the reassurance of the Stealth semi-automatic in my hand.

I tried to stand, and after two awkward attempts I was back on my feet. My knees quivered and my hands shook. I stood in the deep brush swaying slightly, listening anxiously for the sound of the Jeep, but there was no sound except my own ragged breathing. With my fingers gripping the handle of the gun, I moved slowly toward the direction of the road. Twigs snapped under each step I took.

Once on the road I headed toward the main house, limping painfully from my injured ankle. I continued to fight the nausea of fear. The road was in poor condition from little use and a small mound divided the center section from the tire ruts. Grass and weeds punctuated the sand and gravel base making my progress slow and awkward.

I whirled toward the sound of his voice.

"I knew all I had to do was be patient," he said, pointing the flashlight beam directly into my face."

He lunged viciously toward me, grabbing my throat and in a single motion he lifted me off my feet with one hand.

I struggled to speak, but I couldn't get the words past my constricted throat, his hand squeezing the very breath out of me. He dragged me across the gravel road by my neck, while I flailed against the attack in violent objection.

In a split second I trapped his hand, pinning it to my throat with my left hand, bringing my right hand up below his elbow as I stepped back to extend his arm. There was an audible pop as his elbow dislocated.

He was cursing and swinging wild merciless blows to my face with his left hand catching me on the jaw knocking me solidly to the ground.

He screeched, "You fuckin' bitch! I'm gonna' kick your ass."

I sprang to my feet and faced him, "Bring it on, fucker!" I hissed.

He kicked out in my direction solidly catching my shoulder and knocking me to the ground.

"I'm going to cut your fingers off one by one. And when I'm done, I'm gonna BBQ them and have them for dinner, while you watch," he laughed grimly.

He kicked out again this time missing my head when I flattened my torso to the ground.

With the agility of a practiced athlete, I scrambled to my feet, kicked him directly in the jaw with a side thrust kick. I tried to put distance between me and his rage. I heard his ragged breath. The flashlight had gone black. I couldn't tell whether he was behind me or in front of me.

Suddenly, the dreaded light from the flashlight once again found my face.

Three shots exploded toward the light and I watched as the beam fell from my eyes to my feet. Free from his hand, the flashlight rolled unhindered on the ground, creating eerie gyrating shadows. I was unable to move toward the body, or back away from it. The darkness, a temporary shroud, the gun still warm in my hand. Turning I found myself in his arms.

"There's two of them," I barked my voice harsh from fear and trauma.

I buried my head in his chest and tried to catch my breath. His embrace was easy and natural.

"Do you know them?" Luka asked.

"No. I've never seen either of them before in my life."

"No Hayes Benton?"

"No," I said. "Definitely, no Hayes Benton."

Luka pulled a walkie talkie from his belt.

"Dad, yeah, Dad. Where are you and the boys at?"

The radio crackled with static, temporarily eclipsing his Father's end of the conversation.

"Lori and I are about a half mile down the road from the cabin. You can't miss us, we're right in the middle of the road."

I heard Mr. Neilson swear loudly, "We got a dead guy up here, Luka. The SOB took a couple shots at us as we were coming up the road."

"For Christ sakes, are you okay?" Luka asked.

"Yeah, yeah. But this unwelcome visitor isn't doing too good, he's got a bullet between the eyes."

"Have you called the sheriff?"

300

"Okay, well I think you best call him now. We got a dead body down here, too."

In less than five minutes Mr. Neilson and three of the ranch hands were standing with us in the middle of the road, each with a rifle balanced easily over their arm. Two of them held camp lanterns.

The headlights from the Denali 4x4 illuminated the bloodied body laying just off the road.

"Make sure nobody touches anything or leaves a bunch of footprints around the body. Got it? We can't disturb anything. The forensics guys will want to see it as pristine as we can have it. We don't want any questions about our motives."

"Are you sure we shouldn't try CPR on this guy, son?

"Three shots to the chest, Dad. He's way past CPR," Luka said flatly.

"Where's the other one, Dad? You said another one took shots at you and the boys."

"Yeah. That son-of-a-bitch is up where the road splits off to the old loafing shed, laying over the steering wheel. Deader than a doorknob. I gotta' tell you Luka this looks bad. If we weren't named Neilson, I think we'd all find ourselves in the county lock up, tonight while they sort things out."

301

"Sometimes it's good to have friends," Luka said philosophically.

"I got Newsome out of bed. I thought it was best if I called him personally."

Luka kicked a clod of dirt with his boot and looked in my direction but made no attempt to join me.

Exhausted, I found a nearby stump, sat down, hugged myself with both arms and began to rock rhythmically, knowing that finally my wild run was over.

"That's it, folks. Cut. Print. Great job guys," the director enthused. "Let's take a break. We can all use some coffee. Be back and ready to work in say, thirty minutes. We are under some pressure from a storm front coming in."

I turned and smiled as someone from the crew handed me a jacket and a cup of coffee. It looked like it was going to be a long night.

Chapter Twenty Five

Good News

I lowered my head to avoid the glare of the flash bulbs and the microphones. It was a feeding frenzy, and I was chum for the hungry crowd of reporters and cameramen jostling against me, and each other, stealing every molecule of oxygen. I was suffocating. The stench of old cigarette smoke, stale perfume, and twice worn clothes sickened me.

Security surrounding me pushed against the crowd as they forced a path from the limo to the sidewalk. One of the guys, a bulldog of a man, swore at a photographer who had moved in too close and was snapping rapid fire shots of me. I turned, covering my face with my forearm as I was escorted past the fevered eyes of the mob, and the ever-hungry camera's eye.

It was pandemonium as reporters screamed questions, intended to generate an unattractive reaction from me, their microphones in my face as I was rushed past them. It seemed the more I tried to avoid their intrusion the more aggressive the mob became.

At last, I caught sight of my co-stars Josh Hunt, Damen Mathews, and Kerry Evans at the end of the red carpet. The premiere of our new movie, *Confusion,* was starting off with a bang. It looked like it was going to be the surprise hit of the summer. I smiled, knowing we had already started wardrobe fittings for episode two of a planned three-part film series.

Dear Reader,

Thank you for choosing *Chasing The Spider*. I loved writing it, and I am thrilled and delighted that you decided to spend time with Sky, Mateo, Hayes, and Luka.

Please drop me a note and let me know what you thought of the book. Also, if you can make the time, please write a review. I would appreciate it immensely. **Here's the link to the book:** https://www.amazon.com/Chasing-Spider-D-S-Mitchell-ebook/dp/B08GM4R13W/ref=sr_1_1?dchild=1&keywords=chasing+the+spider+d.+s.+mitchell&qid=1603675636&sr=8-1

I'd also like to invite you to visit my website: www.chasingthespider.com where you will find info about me, book updates, and all kinds of free and interesting stuff.

Book Websites:

www.chasingthespider.com

News and Political Websites:

www.calamitypolitics.com

www.calmitynewsandpolitics.com

Coming Spring 2021

Chasing The Spider 2

306

Made in the USA
Monee, IL
17 February 2021